Thorp Jones

18/12/004

Judd St.

Vic

EARTHY TONES

A Selection of
Best Punjabi Short Storeis
GURDIAL SINGH
(Jnanpeeth Award Winner)

Translation & Introduction
RANA NAYAR

FiCTiON HOUSE

ISBN : 81-288-0105-8

FIRST ENGLISH EDITION 2002
PUBLISHED BY
S. BALWANT
FOR

A UNIT OF
AJANTA BOOKS INTERNATIONAL
1 UB Jawahar Nagar, Bunglow Road,
Delhi 110007 (INDIA)
Tel : 91-11-3926182, 7415016 Fax -7415016
E mail : <ajantabi@ndf.vsnl.net.in>
ajantabi@id.eth.net

PRINTED IN INDIA AT
D.G. Printers
Shahdra, Delhi-32

Contents

Introduction

Much before I came to read Gurdial Singh's stories, I had known him only as a novelist. My introduction to him as a novelist was also a fortuitous one. I had translated a few stories from Punjabi and was scouting around for a publisher. My colleague and friend, Pushpinder Syal, happened to mention this fact to the editor of Macmillan India whom she had met during one of the conferences. Around that time, Macmillan India was working out the finer details of a series called Modern Indian Novels in Translation, a massive, five-year long project whereby fifty-five novels were to be translated and published from as many as eleven Indian languages. Expressing her inability to publish the stories, the editor had, by way of a counter-proposal, suggested that they would certainly be interested if someone were to translate a well-known Punjabi novel into English. That is how Pushpinder and I had ended up collaborating on *Addh Chanini Raat* (called *Night of The Half-Moon* in its English rendering), a Sahitya Akademi Award winning novel of Gurdial Singh. Of all the major living writers in Punjabi, how and why the choice had ultimately narrowed down to Gurdial Singh is, of course, part of another much longer story.

Suffice it is to say here that translating Gurdial Singh's fiction was an extremely gratifying, though not a less challenging, experience. Perhaps, it was so gratifying only because at every juncture it threw up new and entirely unexpected challenges. His fiction has this unerring tendency to knock a translator, a professional more than an amateur, completely out of his complacence. There is something about Gurdial Singh's fiction, which doesn't submit itself readily to an act of translation, and least of all, to an English translation. In a way, the challenge is inherent in the fact that Punjabi and English don't merely represent two distinct, not necessarily antithetical, languages or linguistic systems but two different cultural worlds as well. It is another matter that both these languages are known to have shared a common ancestry in Indo-European family of languages and started evolving almost around the same time. Though there might have been a historical contiguity about the growth of these two languages, it is also a fact that, in the process of their evolution, both have followed a markedly different trajectory. Despite the fact that Punjabi literature has had as long a tradition of writing as that of English; for a variety of historical reasons, Punjabi language has definitely not grown at the same pace and has not had as much of a spread as has English.

Right through its long, arduous journey, the tradition of Punjabi writing, which easily dates back to the medieval times or say, 12th century AD, is believed to have maintained a vital, living contact with a much older oral tradition. However, it is not at all easy to map out this relationship as it has presumably run its own distinctive course in different genres available in Punjabi. Even without going into its intricacies, which would undoubtedly call for a much larger discussion, one may safely suggest that almost all the Punjabi writers have sought to negotiate this oral/written, linguistic/literary space in their own distinctive manner. However, in case of Gurdial Singh, this particular relationship takes on a very specific form; it surfaces as an unfailing insistence upon the spoken word. Being firmly rooted in the soil, he never quite fails to bring alive the natural rhythm and resonance of the spoken word. While this lends to his portrayal of situations and characters a rare authenticity and dramatic urgency, it also imparts to his fiction a certain quality of earthiness, even classical charm and simplicity. Largely recognised as one of the strengths of Gurdial Singh's art of fiction- making, it is this quality which may often turn out to be a major source of anxiety for his translator(s).

In my early encounters with Gurdial Singh's fiction, it was

this challenge of having to render into English the speech of his rustic characters, with all its inflections and tonal qualities, that both enthralled and teased me at the same time. Had it simply been a question of finding English equivalencies for the local idiom used by his characters, it wouldn't have really mattered so much. Translation, as any translator worth his salt would easily concede, is not merely a game of finding linguistic equivalencies at the semantic or the syntactic levels. Often the local idiom is so deeply embedded in the cultural layers that any attempt at a simple rendering could, at best, turn into a contraction or a reduction and at worst, a deflection, if not a total loss of meaning. Besides, the syntactic structures in the two languages viz., Punjabi and English operate so very differently that often the process of transmission from one to the other may threaten to become obfuscating, even non-communicative. Whichever way we choose to think about it, the loss is invariably of those cultural specificities that are intrinsically and inherently resistant to any act of translation, howsoever shrewd or strategic. While self-reflexivity is an inescapable fact of any translator's job, it doesn't always become a route to self-awareness. Even in those cases where it does become so, the practise of translation may often throw up challenges which no amount of anticipation or awareness might actually be able to help tide over. Faced with some of these limitations, the task of a translator, especially if he is seeking to capture the 'spirit of the original,' may actually become not easy but all the more difficult, even formidable.

Now this is certainly not intended to be a catalogue of a translator's woes, though it just might appear to be so. The real purpose behind this exercise is neither to find alibis for a certain quality of translation, nor to justify it. On the contrary, it is to focus on some of those qualities of Gurdial Singh's fiction, which may legitimately be accessed only through the interactive mode of translation. While working my way through his novels, (apart from *Night of the Half-Moon*, *Parsa* is another of his novels that I have translated) what really struck me about Gurdial Singh's fiction was its finely crafted minimalism, which undoubtedly has a rare sculptor's touch. This minimalism is evident not only in the way in which he designs the mise-en-scene of his novels but also in the selection of his subject matter, his skilful, deft use of the language and his microscopic vision of life. The real strength of his fiction, it appears to me, doesn't lie so much in creating larger than life images but in crafting living monuments out of the ordinariness of our lives and the inanities we often find appalling, if not disgusting. A true miniaturist, he often applies small, finely tuned strokes, making capital out of the moments we either tend to forget or are rather dismissive about. 'Arching of an eyebrow' or 'twitching of a lip' or 'rippling of the calf-muscles' are not simply physical gestures in Gurdial Singh's fictional repertoire. These are, in fact, the very soul and substance of a man's inner world, signs that reveal the seething ruptures in his soul, authorial interventions into the little known realm of his character's unconscious. He believes in paring his language down to its bare essentials, pruning away the excesses with the ease of a meticulous craftsman. Unsparingly self-critical in his use of the language, he is almost poignantly economical and thrifty. A hallmark of his classicism and often a critical reader's delight, this thriftiness might, in a manner least suspected, turn into a translator's nightmare, too.

Nowhere does this aspect of Gurdial Singh's writing become so transparently conspicuous as in his short fiction. For someone whose self-chosen calling is that of a minimalist, short fiction certainly does provide unlimited possibilities. And without a doubt, one could say that he has, over the decades, explored all these possibilities to their utmost, as stories in the present collection would easily bear out. One of the trenchant ironies of literary history is that Gurdial Singh has earned almost all of his plaudits as a novelist, while he is known to have written some of the most memorable of the stories in Punjabi. Much before he turned to novel as his chosen medium of expression, he had kick started his literary career by writing short stories, a romance which has apparently outlived his love affair with the novel. He continues to write short fiction and already has something like eight collections of stories to his credit, out of which *Saggi Phul* (1962), *Upra Ghar* (1966), *Kutta Te Admi* (1972), *Begana Pindh* (1981) and *Kareer Di Dhingri* (1991) could easily be cited as the more popular ones. In a way, it is his success in long fiction that could be seen to have obscured, if not eclipsed, his several attainments in the realm of short story. Often it is believed and rightly so, that novel and short story, despite being soul mates, incarnate themselves into bodies as different as could be. Put simply, though both are actuated by a common desire to narrate a story, a novelist may be said to enjoy a certain advantage, which may even be seen as a handicap by some, of working within the rambling fictional space that is just not available to a short fictionist. The difference in terms of the demands these two genres make upon their respective practitioners could, in a way, be seen as something analogous to that between one artist choosing to work upon a large sheet of canvas, and another, giving expression to his creativity upon a grain of rice. Gurdial Singh belongs to that rare breed of fiction makers who could be said to move in and out of both forms of fiction, long and short, with the same amount of ease and felicity. It is another matter that his discerning readers have always been quick to admire the born story-teller in him, one who sometimes does make a conscious effort to hide behind the mask of a novelist.

It was this desire to unmask the real face of the master story teller behind an extremely popular and well known Punjabi novelist that, in fact, prompted me to undertake the present assignment. To say the least, it has, indeed, been a sheer delight to discover this other, relatively little known face of Gurdial Singh. That this face has been known to a vast cross-section of Punjabi readership for decades is hardly a consolation. With the exception of a few of his stories, which have been translated and published in newspapers and literary journals, the major gamut of his work is still not available in English. The present collection is the first concerted attempt at making Gurdial Singh's short fiction available in translation to a much larger reading public than has had access to it until now. If translation is about cross-cultural traffic among languages, it is equally about discovering different facets of a writer's work as well. It is with this in mind that the selection of the stories has essentially been done. Undoubtedly, it has not been an easy task to choose fourteen stories from among a range of a few hundred that form an integral part of Gurdial Singh's oeuvre. And the selection has been done in such a manner that the repetition of a style, theme or an idea is scrupulously avoided. How far I have actually succeeded in my intent to, not simply render, but make Gurdial Singh available in English is something each reader must decide for himself or herself.

Among other things, it is also intended that this anthology would help in debunking some of the popular notions about Punjabi literature in general and Gurdial Singh's fiction in particular. For instance, it is often believed, for whatever reason, that Gurdial Singh's range is severely limited as he chooses to restrict himself to the portrayal of village life and rural-based characters. There is no doubt that his fiction is, by and large, village-centred but it would be wrong to assume that it fails to cross its self-imposed boundaries. A typical Indian or a Punjabi village is no longer an insulated place or a haven that can't be intruded upon or penetrated. Its boundaries have already been breached and violated. Assailed by an invisible threat of urbanism, the village is perceived to be redefining its relationship with its cultural 'other' as well as its own exclusionist identity. And this is something that Gurdial Singh knows with insights only an insider can possibly have. Set in an undefined urban location, *A Season of No Return* is an extremely sensitive exploration of the psychological changes that often result from this unequal interaction between the village and the town. Kauri comes to live with her son to help her daughter-in-law through her period of confinement. In total defiance of stereotypical characterisation, Santokh, her son, is shown to be a perfect picture of obedience and so is her daughter-in-law. Both are more than willing to do their duty by her and yet somewhere deeper inside, Kauri is not comfortable with herself. Santokh and his wife do attend to each and every physical needs of hers, including the most minor ones, yet are completely oblivious to her deeper, emotional needs as much as they are of their own. Caught in a circular motion, they seem to have made a habit of leading a jejune, clockwork life, which Kauri finds so intolerable that she constantly yearns to join her husband back in the village. What ultimately snaps the thread for her is the crass, commercial attitude of her son, who decides to send her back only when her physical condition worsens. It is within such a frame of interpersonal relationships that Gurdial Singh seeks to put much larger questions in focus for us.

The Watch Isn't Working Anymore is another story in this collection which deals with how the winds of change sweep through the village, rather surreptitiously, ripping apart its secure and stable network of relationships. Kunda is a retired army personnel who has raised his only son, Kelu, by mortgaging the only piece of land he had. On being pointed out by people that it was a mistake on his part to do so, he retorts, "Property has meaning only so long as people are around." It is around this simple belief that he has built his entire life, and what is much worse, he treats his personal belief as the only barometer of all human relationships. Unknown to him, his son has already discarded this value system and moved on ahead. Educated and employed in a town, he now lives by an entirely new code in which visiting home is more of a ritual, not an expression of love; and the only way to express feelings is to bring his father out-of-ordinary, expensive gifts. The manner in which Gurdial Singh has tried to capture the child-like excitement and enthusiasm of an old father is certainly a comment on his characterisation, stamped as it is with rare sensitivity and psychological depth. The same 'watch' which had made Kunda feel that he was ahead of others in the village ultimately leaves him in a time-warp. On being denied the simple joy of participating in his son's wedding, Kunda feels that the watch has stopped working for him, and that he has been left way behind in the onward flow of time.

In *A House with Two Rooms*, however, the focus is entirely urban, both in terms of location and characterisation. A grim and sordid drama of urban nightmare that often runs so close to our lives, regardless of whether we live in a mofussil town or a metropolis, is what unfolds before our eyes as the story progresses. Nameless characters belonging to a lower middle class family live out their cramped, pigeon holed existence in two drab, cheerless rooms. Seen through the eyes of a retiringly passive husband, it's an extremely graphic account of how, despite all the good intentions on his part, his repeated attempts at spending a holiday quietly by himself, reading, are doomed to failure. On the face of it, it might seem to be the handiwork of his overbearing and shrewish wife, the hesitant, financial demands of his young, adolescent though loving daughters and a quiet but disturbing presence of his old, ailing father. But the real culprit, it turns out, is the oppressively limited space, which constantly throws them across each other's path and yet fails to bring them together in any real sense. Somewhat like the inhabitants of Dante's *Inferno,* each one of them remains locked up in a painful awareness of his/her own condition. And the extent to which their loneliness has left them dehumanised is not revealed until the old father ultimately dies. Often, in his portrayal of urban angst, Gurdial Singh goes so far in search of an apt metaphor that he almost begins to remind one of Baudelaire and Eliot.

Among others, it's in *The Dam, Silent Rage, A Black Bull, The Cattle Fair* and *A Haunted House* that Gurdial Singh returns to his familiar locale, a village, in a more explicit way. So evocative is his picture of a typical Punjabi village that even those amongst us who have never been inside a village somehow begin to feel that we have lived, at least, part of our lives there. The sights, sounds and smells are, of course, all there but more significantly, so are the warning signals of the dangers a village is often exposed to, both from within and without. It's the imminent threat of flood looming large over a small, unprotected village that becomes thunderously real in *The Dam*. The story seems to suggest that this kind of threat can still be guarded, if not managed or fought against. From this perspective, the lone image of Pakhar keeping a vigil in the fields through the dark, ominous night, indeed, becomes unforgettably heroic. What Gurdial Singh is actually at pains to point out is there is another kind of a threat as well, equally real and perhaps more dangerous, that is slowly corroding away the very edges of our social life. And this threat either comes from the local politicians out to exploit the situation or the administrators, revelling in their own apathy. It has become such an integral part of our lives that we don't even see it as a threat any longer.

Not the one to simply bemoan this fact, Singh prefers to use short story as a medium for sensitising his readers about the issues that already are affecting or are likely to affect their lives, directly or indirectly. There is a definite revolutionary potential in his stories that no discerning reader can afford to miss. At one level, *The Cattle Fair* may appear to be a purely descriptive story, giving a first hand account of an insider's view of an annual, village fair. At another subtler level, however, it is about the imperceptible, though not entirely an implausible, process of psychological transformation. Two illiterate brothers, Santu and Pala, who have never perceived themselves as distinct from cattle, set out to see the fair. At least, one of them returns home, changed. After having borne the tyranny and oppression of his own father for several years, he now decides to raise a banner of revolt against him. The message that comes through loud and clear is that regardless of where and in what form it is found, home or outside, father or politician, oppression must always be fought and resisted.

Nothing appears to disturb Gurdial Singh so much as does the prospect of abject surrender that human beings often make to their situations or circumstances. Resistance appears to be a key word in his creative vocabulary and it is this mantra of resistance that he recites in one story after another. Sometimes, it takes on a visibly disturbing image of Bhunda, the dumb one, rushing headlong into revenge with little or no thought to the consequences as in

Silent Rage. And sometimes, it becomes a revolting though pathetic image of an able-bodied Attra moping over his fate, crying out in despair and helplessness, "Why did you send me on this earth as a man? It would have been much better to be born a bull," as in *A Black Bull*. However, if neither the sociology of resistance is grasped fully nor the enemy identified clearly, as it happens to be the case with Melu in *A Haunted House*, then, sanity is the price that one may have to pay for it. It is no coincidence that most of those who are perceived to be the agents of resistance in Gurdial Singh's short stories also happen to be sharing an inalienable relationship with their soil. It is almost as if the village, shorn of its over-romanticised image, stands transformed into the ultimate battleground for resistance in all its myriad forms. Equally, it is seen as a fertile soil for some of the worst human evils, imaginable. Almost all the stories appear to scream out that the acts of human deception, treachery or machinations are as common here as elsewhere. Gurdial Singh's interest in village, its life and people does not merely perform a sociological function as is often assumed, but has a definite transcendent function, too. Put simply, he tends to view it as a microcosm of the world where all kinds of human conflicts and predicaments could and do play themselves out. Such an element of universalism is what mostly accounts for the timeless appeal of his short fiction.

Among other things, Gurdial Singh has often been criticised for not giving enough space in his fiction, long as well as short, to the representation of women. It is believed not only among his Punjabi readers but also his long-time critics that women simply hover on the fringes of his fiction. Neither do they manage to grab the centre-stage of action nor do they ever come vibrantly alive. It has also been argued that being primarily a male-centred writer, he just doesn't understand the psyche of women. And that often, for this very reason, he fails to do justice by women characters as and when he does venture out to create any. While finalising the present collection, special care was given to the fact that stories dealing with women-centred themes were given almost as much space as the others. On a closer scrutiny, it'll be found that as many as five stories included in this selection not only tend to see things from the perspective of women but also focus exclusively upon their inner, private world. It is hoped that the present collection would, to some extent, at least, succeed in giving a lie to, if not in nailing, most of the prejudices and misconceptions that have, over the years, grown around Gurdial Singh's fiction. While translating *The Kareer Branch*, I was particularly struck by the rare sensitivity and psychological insight with which Singh has created Balwanto's character. Naturally rebellious and fiercely independent, Balwanto finds herself in some kind of a psychological trap when her husband manages to get a promise out of her that, whatever the provocation, she would never ever raise her voice in presence of his parents. Stuck in her throat like a thorny bush of *kareer*, this promise keeps lacerating her inner being, corroding its edges and soaking up natural sap, for eleven long years. Once famous in the entire village for her incomparable beauty, she slowly begins to wilt and wither. And one day, when the thread of her supreme patience finally snaps, out leaps *Kalka Mai,* thirsting for revenge. In the hands of a lesser writer, the story would have become another variation on a stereotypical torture-and-revenge theme, but not so with Gurdial Singh. It is his fine understanding of human mind and motivations, which ultimately enables him to go beyond the expectations of an ordinary reader. Though one may have reservations about the final resolution of the story, it is hard not to agree with the contention that Balwanto is caught in a classic, ageless conflict which neither permits her to live with the promise nor without it. The complexity of her predicament lies in the fact that she neither wants to be untrue to herself nor her husband. Her suffering has something almost Grecian about it, and so has her tragedy.

If it is subversive patriarchy that seems to work against Balwanto, Maghar's wife in *Price of a Bride* is shown to be a victim, not of a system, but of another woman's jealousy. Led into believing that Maghar's wife is the one responsible for ensnaring her own husband, Santi undergoes a rapid transformation from a loving, affectionate wife into a cranky, die-hard nag. Interestingly enough, she doesn't quite understand the reasons for this dramatic change in her own temperament. Initially, she directs all her venom against her husband but when that doesn't help the matters much, she throws Maghi's wife out of the house, only to regret her decision later. Driven by her blind, unidentifiable impulses, Santi becomes both a helpless victim and a repentant victimiser. In *Ambo*, however, we find Gurdial Singh talking about a strange kind of sorority that develops between two women, one old and authoritarian, and the other young and fragile, both of whom have a purely chance encounter in the compartment of a train. Thrown together into proximity, which both find rather hateful and revolting in the beginning, slowly they grow into a better understanding of each other, even of their own selves. Not only this, the younger one who had always been something of a coward, finds sudden tidal waves of confidence surging up inside her. What is, indeed, remarkable is that so much happens without too many words passing between the two of them. The success of the story is as much in the subtle manner in which Gurdial Singh makes both women catalysts' of each other's inner change as it is in his ability to twist this astonishingly ordinary human situation into one of extraordinary, philosophical interest. Going beyond its immediate appeal, it turns into an extended reflection upon the age-old, philosophical question of how and in what possible ways could mind and body interact and influence each other.

To bring philosophy out of the closet and into our lives is something that does call for very special narrative skills on part of any writer. And no less skilful or formidable is the task of portraying, no, not the sentimental, calf love of the adolescent or the youth (of which there is no dearth in world fiction) but a calm, serene or mature feeling that grows between two persons, equally helpless and vulnerable. *Bonding* is about how, sometimes, sharing a few moments with a person one has loved and lost could be much more meaningful than an entire loveless life spent together. Though Bantu and Jai Kaur meet at the station unexpectedly and part soon after, their silhouettes framed against the setting sun or wending their way slowly to the village, remain etched on our minds, forever. What is, indeed, praiseworthy is that their meeting is refreshingly free of sudden, hysterics of emotion, painful reminders of the broken promises and 'you-failed-me or I-failed-you' kind of recrimination. Surprisingly, there is a lingering suspicion, a strange inability to trust someone who had made 'trust' possible in the first place. A bond buried in time is resurrected temporarily and it leaves behind, not a trail of nostalgia but, a strange fulfilment that only a deep bonding could possibly yield. Behind this ability to handle a seemingly volatile situation with utmost restraint and control, one could easily detect the hand of a master craftsman. Though certainly not as powerful as some others, *The Topmost Bough* and *In my Own Hand*, too, may be said to have their own distinctive flavour, which is recognisably Gurdial Singh's.

In the ultimate analysis, the only yardstick of a writer's success or failure is the reader's response to his work. I do hope that this collection of his stories in translation will go, at least, part of the way towards creating a very special affection for Gurdial Singh in the hearts of his English speaking readers. Well, if it does succeed in doing so, it might be said that this anthology has served some real purpose. And if it doesn't, the blame is entirely mine for not having been able to render his fiction into English with as much ease as he commands in his original writing.

Rana Nayar
Chandigarh
May, 2002

The Watch Isn't Working Anymore!

All of a sudden, one day Kelu returned to the village. No letter, no message; no intimation either. Though he did want to shoot off several questions, yet the moment Kunda set his eyes upon Kelu in the dim light of the lantern, he forgot almost everything he wanted to ask him. Seeing a huge turban tied upside down and an unkempt beard, as long as the tail of a falcon, he came across as some kind of a 'sardar'. Then seeing his olive-green, checked shirt, three-four inches wide leather-belt around the waist and trousers with flair, as loose as the bottoms of a salwar, Kunda could barley suppress his smile between his moustaches.

"*Bai*, what on earth do you look like, really?" said he with a smile, "It appears as though you have returned from *Amreeka* just now."

"Why, do I look that strange?" asked Kelu in surprise, twisting around to look at his clothes somewhat self-consciously.

Kunda kept quiet. On hearing this about himself, Kelu was not in the least surprised. Kunda, too, felt as though he hadn't really welcomed the boy the way he ought to have. So, in order to make up, he started inquiring after his health.

After some time when Kelu took a square-looking pocket watch and a double-edged staff out of his holdall and handed them in, Kunda kept staring at both the things for a long time. Then giving them back to him, he said, "Keep them with you. We'll see in the morning. You can hardly see anything in the dark."

Stuffing the watch and the staff back into his bag, Kelu started talking about his job. As long as Kelu's mother Jinta was busy preparing a meal for him, both the father and the son kept up the tenor of their own gossip.

Kelu was working in an oil-refinery at Bombay. After two years, he had been promoted and sent to Assam. As he had been given ten days of joining time, he had come home to meet his parents.

"I just thought that it may take me, God alone knows, how long to come home again. Now they have really sent me to a far-off place. That's why I thought of visiting my village." Kelu offered a long-winded explanation.

"You did the right thing. Good, in a way." Kunda spoke without concealing his happiness, "As if it is easy to come from such a far-off place!"

Kelu's *bebe* softly whispered in a voice choked with sentiment, "Kelu, my son! Is it not possible for you to get yourself transferred somewhere nearer home?"

"If they're able to dig up oil somewhere around, then it might be possible, not otherwise."

How was the poor *bebe* to know where and how the oil was to be found? She just took a deep sigh and kept quiet.

The next morning Kunda got ready, put on his freshly starched turban and clearing up his throat said, "Where is it? Let's see now what that watch really looks like."

Bringing both the things from inside, Kelu handed them in to his father. Holding it in his hand, his father first scrutinised the watch very carefully. For a long time, he kept staring at the square-looking, ebony-dark box. The box had flowers embossed in copper (or perhaps gold) in all the corners. Right in the middle of the box, in a space less than a thumb impression, was imprinted a golden image of a peacock. The peacock had spread its feathers in all its majestic glory. The feathers, the neck and the crown of the peacock had been painted in the colours that almost made it look like a real bird. Kunda's eyesight was fairly good. He could even spot gems, as big as a *khas* grain, where the eyes of the peacock should have been. Running his hands over its eyes, he felt as though he were touching the eyes of a real peacock.

After a while, pushing the watch towards Kelu, he asked, his face breaking into a broad smile, *"Bai*, how do you open it?"

Taking the watch from him with a smile, Kelu thumbed open a white button that lay towards the top left. With a cracking sound, the box split open into two triangular portions. Even the peacock split into two. When Kunda saw the bright hands of the watch staring back at him from its squirt, sparkling steel frame, he jumped in amazement. Then Kelu explained to him how, by using a button at one end, he could turn around the hands to set the watch or wind it, whichever way he wanted to. The watch had a long chain with the help of which it could easily be tucked inside the *kurta* pocket. And then he told his father how to tuck it inside the buttonhole with a ring that lay attached to the chain. Almost like a child, Kunda kept asking him about everything time and again as though he were doing something extraordinary.

For three days, Kelu stayed at home. And all the three days, Kundu kept the watch and the staff in a trunk, under lock and key. Time and again, he felt tempted to sneak a look at both the things but in Kelu's presence; it would have appeared to be somewhat childish.

On the fourth day when Kelu was about to leave, he bowed to his mother and said, "All right, *bebe,* I'll try and come again in another four to five months. So don't worry."

"What's there to worry?" Kunda spoke rather confidently, "You're going back to a job, after all. And for a job, people are ready to go as far as China, even beyond! ...May you earn well and lead a peaceful life. Why should we worry!"

It was only to put the her weight behind his words that she said, her voice choking over with emotion, "May you always be happy! Who knows, you just might be transferred to a place nearer home some day…"

Though something had nearly cracked inside Kunda, he put on a brave front and said, "Never you mind. May *Waheguru* bestow His blessings upon you…Next year when we marry you off, you must take long leave and come home. That would really please your mother."

On hearing this bit about his marriage, the tear-stained eyes of Biro suddenly lit up. But Kelu did not say anything.

*   *   *

The very next day, Kunda took a small piece of *khaddar* and went to Faggan, the tailor. Faggan started talking about Kelu. But getting somewhat impatient, Kunda said, "First let me tell you what has to be done to the *kurta*…"

"All right, tell me!" spoke Faggan somewhat sarcastically, his buckteeth showing through his straggly beard, "What'll you tell me that collars are to be stitched here or cuffs with studs made there – *henh?*"

"*Oye*, Faggana, you shouldn't really talk nonsense all the time – time is of utmost importance, after all."

"Really!" Concealing his upper row of scattered teeth behind his moustache and simulating a serious expression on his face, he said, "It's all right. I'm being careful now. So, tell me, what's to be done?"

While giving instructions about the piece of cloth and the way it was to be stitched inside the *kurta* almost as if it was a double pocket, Kunda cleared his throat with such earnestness that Faggan began to sense trouble. With great effort, he fought back the words that were forming on his lips, "So, are you making the final preparations now?" But seeing Kunda's dead pan expression, he dared not utter a single word.

On the fourth or the fifth day, when Kunda walked into the village assembly wearing a new *kurta*, a new *pyjama* and sporting a white muslin turban, a staff in hand, his friends just stared blankly at his pocket watch and the staff.

Taking the staff off his hands and sizing him from head to toe, Rattan Bhinder said, "Now you've become a real pensioner!" As he loosened the handle of the staff, it split open and almost six inches long leather-cloth between the two parts stretched itself taut, much in the manner of a resting chair.

"*Bai*, what's this?" asked Khema, as he stared at the staff, wide-eyed, "O you respectable one, this has really turned into a little chair!"

"Yes!" Taking the staff from Rattan's hands and pressing down the leather-cloth, he passed it on to Khema saying, "If you feel tired while walking, all you have to do is to fix it into the ground and sit upon it. You can always rest upon it a little. Then fold it up like this, before you go along your way merrily!"

With these words, Kunda lifted both the portions of the staff and it became a stick again. And that leather-cloth was concealed within. Almost everyone from the old to the middle-aged, down to the youngsters kept staring at the staff in sheer amazement. Looking somewhat like an ebony dark snake, it had such a sturdy silver support that even if someone as heavy Famman, who was no less than a hundred and sixty kilos, were to put all his weight upon it, it wouldn't shake or quaver in the least. Everyone took turns to ask Kunda, again and again, "O respectable one! What kind of wood is it?"

Keeping quiet, Kunda just shook his head for some time. Then feeling proud, he cleared his throat and started right from the beginning in a solemn tone, "This wood is found up in the hills. And its tree is sometimes as tall as fifty feet...Besides, its branches…"

And he took a long time to finish his story. The old men believed each and every word spoken by him but the young started smiling all to themselves. While wending his way to the fields, Palu's son Paaru had heard everything. He laughed and said, "*Tayya,* which Sumeru mountain does our Kelu live on?"

Seeing a mischievous expression in Paaru's eyes, Kunda stared at him and said, "Yes, he lives on the one that is on your mother's head."

Everyone started laughing at Kundu's peevishness. Paaru, too, had a hearty laugh and went off towards the fields.

Then for a long time, all kinds of stories about the square pocket watch and the double-edged staff of Kunda kept doing the rounds of the village. Everyone was envious of him though almost everyone had a good word for his praiseworthy son Kelu. Most of all, it was Rattan Bhinder who touched upon the same subject each time he met Kunda.

"It's all destiny, Kunda Singh!" Heaving a deep sigh, he said, "The good deeds of your previous birth are catching up with you now. But where should we go and drown ourselves? Bloody, all four of them are always ready to pounce on me. As long as I was in good health, they didn't really mind the old man around the house. Now they don't even bother to offer a glass of sour *lassi* to me...Anyway, see you another time...it's all a matter of time. Perhaps it was in my fate to witness all this."

In a bid to reassure him a little, Kunda said, "Don't you worry. I'll try and explain it to them! O silly fool! If we've grown old, it doesn't really mean that they should discard us and give us away to the junk-dealer the way you do it with the old, worn-out machinery? They shouldn't really do it. After all, won't they have to face this tomorrow?"

Everyone was surprised how Kundu had now started using a smattering of English as well. That is why rank and file had begun to hold him in great awe.

Around the same time, another unusual thing happened when Kunda started talking in terms of securing the release of the land he had mortgaged. While sending Kelu off to college, he had had to mortgage four acres of land out of the thirteen he owned, something that had really made him lose face within the community. People had rushed in with all kinds of suggestions but Kunda had refused to change his stance. Regardless of what people had to say, he just went ahead and financed Kelu's education. And when his son got himself a job, Kunda decided to give his land on contract and became a 'pensioner' himself. So much so that people started calling him 'Kunda Pensioner'. Some people would also address him as 'Kunda Singh Sahib'.

When Kunda had returned from the army, Kelu was barely four years old. He was reeling under the burden of marrying off three girls, all of whom were older to Kelu. He was the only earning member and had about thirteen acres of land. He had worked tirelessly, day and night, becoming one with the soil. Almost for fifteen years, he had remained in a virtual state of exile. Once his daughters had been married off and Kelu, too, having finished his studies had found himself a job and got engaged to the daughter of a reasonably well to do farmer, he somehow felt that all his labour had really been well worth it. So much so that he hadn't really felt in the least embarrassed about mortgaging his land.

"Property has meaning only as long as people are around!...It's people who create property. If fortune favours them, they'll be able to create it for themselves. Otherwise, what do I need all this for? All I need are two square meals a day. And for that my pension money is more than enough. I don't really need any property!" He would often argue with people around.

Even those people, who had earlier treated his arguments as the wishful thinking of a dreamer, now seeing a change in his fortunes, had begun to wonder, even started feeling somewhat jealous of him in a way. No one in the village had ever seen the kind of watch and the staff that Kunda had in his possession now. The watch showed such an accurate time that everyone from Chaube to Mirab would set their watches by it. While telling them time, he would even look at the hand indicating seconds and say, "It's twenty three minutes past seven and almost thirty seconds!"

It was indeed amazing the way Kunda's watch always showed perfect time. Besides, it was so attractive that he often felt like taking it out of his pocket and looking at it.

Now whenever Kunda had to go to *mandi* (which was quite often) he would quickly go over it in his mind, work out the time it would take him on the way and then start from home at thirty three or four minutes past seven. Resting his hand upon the staff and walking in a leisurely manner, by the time he ambled across to the gate with the lion's mouth, all the shops would be open. The shopkeepers would be busy lighting joss sticks at the threshold of their shops. Standing next to the pillar of the gate, he would first dust off his face, hands and feet, straighten his turban, rest his staff against the pillar, take the watch out of his pocket and press the top-button. It was almost as if the hands of the watch played hide-and-seek with him, making a sudden cracking sound! He would start smiling, as each time it would be five or six minutes to nine – neither less nor more.

*   *   *

One day, Kelu's letter arrived. This one was heavier than the ones he usually sent. On opening it, Kunda found Kelu's photograph inside. Apart from him, it had three or four other boys and girls as well. The girl who was standing next to Kelu, her shoulder touching his, had a full and broad face – the shape of a dung-cake. Though she was short, her body was as tough as that of a wrestler. In the letter Kelu had mentioned that all these boys and girls were his colleagues and friends. Kunda somehow found it rather hard to stomach this bit about his friendship with girls. Then he started reasoning it out on his own, 'It's all right. After all, one has to swim with the current. Even the English used to move around freely with each other – They're all unmarried. So how does it matter what they do.' Despite everything, the strangeness of the photograph had continued to haunt him for quite a few days, thereafter.

After about two months when Kelu's in-laws started sending frantic messages, he decided to send two letters to Kelu, one following the other. But he was rather surprised to find that Kelu hadn't bothered to write back for almost a month. Finally he went to *mandi* and asked one of the sons of the commission-agents to send a reply-paid telegram. When he didn't get a response even on waiting for another four days, it naturally had him worried. Thinking that Kelu might be unwell, he sought his wife's advice in the matter, expressing his keenness to visit him for

a few days. It was while he was still preparing to leave that Kunda
received Kelu's letter. An envelope again — almost as heavy as
the one he had received earlier. On opening it, he saw that it had
a photograph wrapped inside a plain paper but there was no letter.
It showed Kelu standing close to the same girl with a broad face,
smiling, bridegroom's *sehra* adorning his head. Even the girl was
dressed up like a regular bride; it also showed how their knot was
inextricably tied.

For a long time, Kunda kept staring at the photograph.
Then he felt as though the smiling face of Kelu was jeering at him.
That very moment, spitting a mouthful of abuse he tore the
photograph off into pieces, threw it into the *chulha*, went and lay
down upon his *manji*. Wiping her smoke-filled eyes, Biro came
up to him and asked repeatedly, "What has Kelu written?" But he
kept lying on the *manji*, without a word. Seeing his condition,
Biro kept walking around him, mumbling things under her breath.

After a while when Sheru Mirab knocked at his door
correct his watch, Kunda had it conveyed to him in a gruff voice,
"Kelu's *bebe*, tell him that the watch isn't working anymore." And
with these words, he started unhooking the chain of the watch
from his buttonhole.

A Season Of No Return

Early in the morning, the daughter-in-law came into the room with a cup of tea in hand and repeated the very same words in her characteristic sweet voice which Kauri had been hearing for the past one year, "Maaji, pranaam! It's six o'clock. Please have your tea."

After leaving the cup on the mat close to her pillow, she went right back, dragging her chappals along. She didn't even bother to see whether or not Kauri had woken up. (It is another matter that she had been lying wide-awake since before the dawn. For almost a week now, she hadn't known what sound sleep was)

Kauri picked up a tumbler of water lying by her side, walked into the bathroom and started washing her hands and face. The daughter-in-law had left a small, neat towel on the peg already. Using it, she wiped her face clean and returned to her room. After having had her tea in small gulps, she lay down again, pulling the blanket over herself. There was hardly anything she could have possibly done. After about twenty minutes or so, she sat up in her manji all over again.

At exactly thirty minutes past six, Santokh walked in, holding kaka in his lap and after greeting her with "Maaji, Sat Sri Akal" he promptly handed him over to her. For a while, at least, her heart danced in joy. Seeing an innocent smile on kaka's face, she felt as though weight had dropped away from her chest. Invoking blessings upon him, she broke into a childish prattle and started conversing with him. Stretching out her hand, she picked up the basket of toys lying on the top of the closet, pulled out a rattle and started shaking it. But every now and then, kaka would get impatient on hearing the tip–tap of his mother's chappals as she went out of her room and into the kitchen or from the kitchen to the bathroom. Looking towards the door, he would start flailing his arms and legs. Then breaking into slow whimpers, he would look up at Kauri's wrinkled face. The moment she noticed a woe-be-gone look on his face, she would start rocking him in the cradle of her arms, making noises such as "hoon-haan-aa-aa…" in an effort to calm him down.

Thus having managed to humour kaka, she would again make him sit in her lap and start conversing with him, "Beeba kaka will take a little duck! He will buy a motor car…he'll drive a car, too!"

And while talking to him, she repeatedly stole a glance towards the kitchen, the daughter-in-law's room, and the bathroom or just stared blankly at the walls, her ears attuned to the sound of the footfalls. (That moment a strange dread could be seen lurking in her eyes).

Suddenly as she felt a wave of nausea sweeping over her, she called out, "San-tok-h! My son…"

"I'm coming, Maaji!" Santokh responded from inside the bathroom. And after a while he came into his mother's room, dressed in spotless, white kurta pyjama, wiping his wet hair with a towel. He looked at kaka and blurted out, "O naughty one, you're up to mischief, again!"

"No, son! I had called out to you so that…"

It was almost as if Santokh had understood her meaning without her having to complete the sentence. So he rushed out, saying, "All right! I'll get the medicine."

That very moment, Kauri had an insistent bout of cough. Santokh returned hastily, a glass of water in hand. Putting down the glass on the mat and taking the medicine out of the strip with the other hand, he handed in a sarson-coloured tablet to his mother. As she put the tablet in her mouth, lifting the glass Santokh offered it to her. Once Kauri had swallowed the tablet down with water, he took the glass from her. Then as he came out, picking up the glass and the wrapper he had removed off the tablet, he whistled, making kaka break into a smile.

Now kaka was happy, playing with the grandmother.

At exact thirty-five minutes past seven, kaka's mummy came into the room, her wet hair spread over her shoulders. Her shapely lips suddenly blossomed into a smile, almost like the petals of a rose. It was as if she was inviting kaka to break into a smile. Then handing in the milk bottle to Kauri she repeated the same sentence she had been spouting at that hour for the past three months now, "Please Maaji, give kaka his feed."

Perhaps, it was the first time in three months that Kauri had not responded with her usual warmth saying, "Give it to me, child". Quietly, she took the feeder and put it to kaka's mouth. Kaka, too, started sucking at it, without a demur. And the daughter-in-law went back, a smile of satisfaction on her lips.

             *   *   *

By quarter past eight, both Santokh and his wife were ready to leave. Going past his mother's room, all Santokh said was, "All right, maaji, we'll make a move now." He went across to the verandah, took his scooter out and kicked hard to start it. Both the husband and the wife sat themselves upon the scooter. That very moment, Kauri came out into the verandah, holding kaka. Both of them raised their hands to say 'ta-ta' to kaka and sped away, smiles pasted upon their faces and their arms swaying through the air. Sucking his left thumb, kaka kept staring at the scooter, wide-eyed. He didn't break into a wail, though.

Kauri kept standing in the verandah for sometime. She was somewhat surprised wondering where was this neighbour, a Gujrati woman, who always used to come out the moment she would hear the scooter leave? That very moment, her neighbour came out; calling out to her from the verandah of her quarter, she spoke in Hindi, "Bheinji, why don't you come over? Are you feeling all right? All well?" Then taking a little breather, she almost screamed as she said, "Bittu, my son, what are you up to? Oye

Bittu! Why don't you come to me?"

Something must have crossed Kauri's mind that she decided not to respond. She just looked at her once, smiled and then adjusting her chunni, walked right back in.

As she came in, kaka had already begun to doze off. She set him down on the bed, and with a little patting he went off to sleep. Getting up, as she went towards the kitchen, again she felt somewhat restive. A huge pile of unwashed dishes lay under the tap. It would be quite sometime before the maid came. But she couldn't possibly touch the dishes. Her son and the daughter-in-law had strictly forbidden her from doing such chores, saying, "Maaji, you must never do such a thing."

Picking up her plate with parantha and curd in it, she came back to her room. As she was about to eat, the very first morsel got stuck in her throat, as it were. With great difficulty, she managed to finish half the parantha. Whatever curd and parantha was left, she covered it with a big plate and put it over the mat. A sudden pain stabbed her back and she lay down towards kaka's feet. For sometime she kept staring at the roof and then her mind started drifting along its own wayward currents.

                    *   *   *

It had almost been a year since she had come here. It was mainly to help her daughter-in-law through her pregnancy. However, this was more of an excuse to find out how attached this daughter-in-law was to her, the one whom her son had married of his own accord, disregarding the wishes of his parents. All their relatives had made a big issue out of it. So much so that she had found it rather difficult to show her face anywhere in the biradari: no marriage procession and no rituals. Who knows which caste she really belonged to but he had insisted on bringing her home and settling in only with her.

After about a year of getting married when Santokh went to the village, no one spoke to him straight. But has anyone been able to separate the flesh from the nails ever? Despite that, Santokh's bapu had suggested somewhat sarcastically, "Bhai, you do whatever you wish to. As if you have ever sought my advice on whatever you've done so far? Don't you worry about me! I could always go to the gurudwara and eat at the langar."

But Santokh's younger brother Gyana was quite pleased with whatever had happened. Right from their childhood, he had always had special affection for Santokh. Pronouncing his judgement, he declared, "Bapu will never talk straight. You take bebe along. We'll manage somehow."

Caught in a dilemma, Kauri had accompanied Santokh, albeit reluctantly. The vision of 'the foreign land' 'thousands of miles away' that she had at the time of leaving home had now been blown to bits ever since she had come here. For a few days, 'this strange land' had almost appeared to be some kind of a paradise to her. Her daughter-in-law, whom everyone condemned as someone of a low caste, would always be around to do her bidding much before she could even spell out her wishes. She wouldn't ever tire of saying 'Maaji, Maaji' all the time. Even at the time of delivery, she had seen to it that maaji was not put to any inconvenience in the hospital. On the night of the delivery when she had insisted on staying back with her, saying, "Come on child! I'm not really going to sleep on the floor here. I'll go and lie down somewhere in the verandah. You never know, you just might need something at night" her daughter-in-law had refused to relent. She had repeatedly told Santokh that he should take her home as she would be inconvenienced there. Even after coming back from the hospital, she had arranged for a maid who could attend to the household chores so long as she was not in a position to do them herself.

Every Sunday, on visiting the gurudwara Kauri would meet up with several Punjabi women. There was a park outside the gurudwara. Sitting there, people would either make new acquaintances or renew the old ones. She, too, had struck a rapport with a woman of her age, who was from Jalandhar. She would often share her joys and sorrows with that woman. Like Kauri, she too had come to be with her son and daughter-in-law.

But once she started bad-mouthing her 'bitch' of a daughter-in-law, Kauri would find it impossible to keep listening to her. On one pretext or the other, she would encourage Kauri to talk of her daughter-in-law as well. She was under the impression that Kauri too would be as sick of her daughter-in-law as she was of her own. Despite her best efforts, when she had failed to get Kauri to talk ill of her daughter-in-law, she began to think of her as 'the blessed one'. By and by, that woman became somewhat envious of her lot as well.

So many times, Kauri wanted that she should rubbish her own daughter-in-law just for the satisfaction of this woman from Doaba. But what should she say? What kind of problem should she talk about?...Both the son and the daughter-in-law were well-placed in their respective jobs: the daughter-in-law was teaching in a college while the son was an engineer in a factory. They had been allotted an official quarter by the government – which was as good as a bungalow. Everything one needs in the house was available at home. In the very first week of her stay, her daughter-in-law had found out all about her needs. Thereafter, she never had to spell out any of her needs. Without having to lift a finger, she would be served everything she required.

Sometimes Kauri would think to herself: what is paradise? Such a wonderful son and a daughter-in-law, a grandson as bright as a moon and a house with plentiful of everything – what more could paradise be?

Still, occasionally she would start feeling rather restive, apparently for no reason whatsoever. In the past two months or so, she had told Santokh several times over, "Kaka, please take me back to the village." But every time he would say the same thing, "What are you going to do there?" Then he would explain to her painstakingly, "I write to Gyana every month. He always writes that bapuji is doing fine – and that bebe should stay here as long as she wishes to. You tell me, are you being inconvenienced here in any way?"

Now what could she say; there was hardly any

inconvenience she could think of. Except that she felt restless occasionally. Sometimes, she just wanted to wing her way back to the village. Such were the moments when her nostalgia for home would grow into a nagging obsession to a point where she would start dreaming of her village at night: the open courtyard of the house and the children frolicking about there – Gyana's son Melu and his daughter Karmi. Their hands dripping with fresh cow-dung, they would be running around the manger, bursting into loud guffaws as they chased each other... Then she would start ranting at them, 'Weh, why don't you stop it now? What kind of a game is it?'

Occasionally when she had such a dream at night, she would start blubbering all to herself, waking up in the process. Drenched in perspiration, she would first glance towards the room of her son and daughter-in-law and then sitting up in her bed, start reciting 'Waheguru-Waheguru' in the darkness of the night.

Sometimes, she would get rather upset about the fact that this place would neither get so unbearably hot in May-June as to make her yearn for endless glasses of cold water nor would it get so cold in the winters as to drive her to sit next to the fire and warm herself. She had asked Santokh many a time as to why the season always remained the same? Laughing it away, he would often say, "Maaji, don't you like this season? People in Punjab must be really yearning for this kind of season that never turns." Once he had explained to her that it was owing to the proximity of the sea that the season remained more or less the same. It had really surprised Kauri to know that there could actually be some connection between the sea and the seasons.

Now everything had begun to appear strange to her, almost like the brown stump of a tree. She no longer liked the sameness of the sweet words her daughter-in-law spoke to her. For the past so many days now each time she came into her room with a cup of tea, tip-tapping her chappals, she would be reminded of her younger daughter-in-law — Gyana's wife. Her dung-cake like face, short statured, stolid body, supple arms and her feet soiled in earth and sand – everything would run before her eyes almost like a movie. That moment she would even get to hear her loud, robust voice – 'Will you come here or not?…Should I teach you a lesson, then?'…And then she would suddenly have a glimpse of both the children cowering behind the chulha. Kauri could even hear the soft voice of her daughter-in-law drifting across as she heaved a basket full of dung-cakes over her head, almost tip-toeing out of the house, saying, "Nee bebeji! Just be careful. Don't let them come after me. There, fighting with each other these two will tear my chunni off."

Lost in such thoughts, Kauri would often break into a spontaneous laughter. Suppressing it between her lips, she would again start staring towards that door of her room, which led to the room of her son and daughter-in-law.

*   *   *

She had been walking around in a daze until she saw the maid coming in, and that is when she felt somewhat relieved. For the past few days, even the maid hadn't appeared to be in her usual frame of mind as she had been going about her work in a rather slipshod manner. Very rarely would she discuss her family matters as she would often rush through her work and push off in a hurry. As it is, she had spread her net so wide that she hardly ever had any time. Often while sweeping the floors or washing the dishes or dusting the tables, when she would suddenly break into a conversation, Kauri invariably found it difficult to tune in to her gibberish and so would keep nodding her head, repeating "All right, all right." As soon as she nodded affirmation, a sudden feeling of peace descended upon her. She wanted to help her out so that after finishing her work in good time, the maid could sit and talk with her. Both of them might be able to share their joys and sorrows. Perhaps, it was the daughter-in-law again who had tutored the maid, for she, too, never allowed her to do a thing. Preventing her from doing the work, she would often screech in Hindi, "Maaji, why do you want to deprive me of my livelihood."

Initially, Kauri used to dislike her immensely. Then she

got to know of her problems. She was the mother of five children. Her husband worked as a coolie at the station. As he squandered all his earnings upon himself, he would not even give a counterfeit coin at home. So she had to earn to provide for her children. Now Kauri had even begun to sympathize with her.

But until today, she had not spoken to the maid properly. As soon as the maid left, kaka woke up. She busied herself with his feed. After the feed when he became engrossed with his own games, she began to heat up her food. Once she had finished her meals, it suddenly occurred to her that kaka was already late for his bath. Giving him a hurried bath, she changed his clothes and washed the old ones as well. In the meanwhile, it was already three o'clock. She gave him another feed on finishing which he went off to sleep.

Overwhelmed by a feeling of emptiness within, Kauri came out into the verandah and sat down there. Having returned from their schools, the children of Gujrati, Bengali and Madrasi families were now busy playing, making noises out in the ground. For a while, at least, she did like their commotion but soon enough, she began to get rather impatient with it. Walking in, she felt as though sweat had soaked her down to the skin. It occurred to her that she hadn't had her bath today. Though she did feel like having a bath, yet somehow she couldn't muster enough strength to walk up to the bathroom.

That very moment she heard the sound of the auto-rickshaw outside and after a while the darling daughter-in-law walked in, her purse dangling across her arms. Flashing a smile in her customary manner, she said "Maaji, pranaam" and then darted a glance towards kaka. Then she shot the same old question, "Did he have his milk properly?" The moment Kauri said "yes" she rushed straight into the bathroom. After a while when she came out, looking at Kauri in a surprised manner, she asked, "Didn't you have your bath today?... You haven't even combed your hair. Go and have your bath — how hot it is!."

At least, momentarily, she was totally befuddled as to how

her daughter-in-law could get to know whether or not she had had her bath. She felt reassured in a rather strange way. It suddenly struck her that she should give a befitting retort saying that she had no intentions of having a bath today. But she held her counsel. Quietly, she walked towards the bathroom. The darling daughter-in-law busied herself with making tea.

At half past five, Santokh came back as well. As was his daily routine, two or three of his friends came with him. After greeting Kauri with a Sat-Sri-Akal, all of them walked into the living room. She could constantly hear the sounds of the peeling laughter and the tip-tapping of her daughter-in-law's chappals coming in from the living room. It felt as though their neighbour's son was firing shots with his air gun. This was enough to make her restless all over again.

At about quarter past six, all of them marched out, perhaps for an evening stroll or for watching a film. She didn't ask any questions. When the darling daughter-in-law came in to pick up kaka, she did mention something about where they were going but the constant buzz in her ears had not really allowed her to hear anything. It was perhaps the roar of the three scooters at a time that made her heart jump into her mouth, as it were. However, once this sound had subsided, the emptiness of the house began to wrap itself around her.

*   *   *

Not having had a wink of sleep the previous night, when Kauri was about to pick up her cup of tea, the next morning, her hands nearly trembled. Falling off her hand, the cup broke into several pieces. Santokh came rushing in. Looking at his mother's face, anxiety gripped him the moment he saw beads of perspiration on her forehead. Kauri was sitting, holding her head between her hands – almost as if her head was swimming. Stepping forward and supporting her shoulders, he said, "Maaji, why don't you lie down." He could feel that her body was somewhat feverish. Lying down, all Kauri said was, "Son, I'm feeling uneasy." That very moment, he got her a tablet and a glass of water. The daughter-in-

law had also come in with him. Both of them helped her sit up and
made her swallow the tablet. After about an hour or so, Kauri felt
much better. Her attention was again drawn towards the room of
her son and daughter-in-law. Hearing Santokh speak in anxious
but soft tones, she pricked her ears and with some effort was able
to hear what he was saying. In a very composed manner, he was
trying to explain it to his wife, "What is the way out now?…Even
I can see the problems it'll create; but we'll engage a maid."

Kauri felt as though her head was swimming all over again.
A sudden feeling of giddiness swept over her. That day, Santokh
took leave and came back home after dropping his wife at college.
On his way back, he brought along a doctor as well. The doctor
examined his mother and told him that there was absolutely nothing
to worry.

By the afternoon, Kauri was feeling somewhat settled.
She had started playing with kaka as well. Santokh sought her
permission and went out. After about two hours when he returned,
he spoke rather softly, "Maaji, I've got your seat booked. It's on
a train leaving next Saturday night. One of our engineers is going
to Punjab. He'll leave you right up to the village."

Kauri was stunned when she heard it. After a while, she
thought of something and said, "Son, it's up to you…if you're
finding it difficult, I won't mind staying a little longer."

"No, it's all right. Now kaka is grown up enough. We'll
manage somehow."

…And until the next Saturday, the whole atmosphere in
the house appeared somewhat sad to her. Though the daughter-
in-law would now speak in a voice sweeter than before and Kauri,
too, would always respond to her quite affectionately; often
Santokh would sit with maaji and crack a few jokes as well – but
everyone could feel that there was something strange and unfamiliar.

That feeling of estrangement and sadness could end only
on Saturday night at seventeen minutes past two. After seeing
maaji off with his friend, when Santokh was returning home he
suddenly felt so cold that his teeth started chattering. He looked

up at the sky; there wasn't a trace of a cloud anywhere around. Then how could it be so cold? The moment he reached home, he joined two blankets and pulled them over himself. After a long time when warmth had seeped inside his body, he felt a sudden lightness of being. Then his thoughts raced back to his mother but a sudden tide of sleep had already washed over him.

...ood day long. Have a cup... anyway... I've got a house on rent,
wait for you to buy...

... The latter was silent. What I had to leave in the car?
...in her nose. She was so close to her...temperature, he would...
...
...
...

A House With Two Rooms

Two incidents had occurred around the same time: one, their son
had left for the big town to appear for an examination; two,
yesterday evening one of their newly acquired *jat* friends Hardev
Singh had taken their dog along. (He said, "I'll take him for a
month as everyday pigs wander into the wheat-fields and ruin the
crop.") That is why the wife had been going around, dazed. And
the third calamity was that it happened to be a holiday. And holiday
is, in any case, a day of sheer troubles for a stay-at-home woman.
On one hand, the children get after her life and on the other, endless
are the demands of the husband. (Besides, he wasn't one of those
'ordinary' husbands. From morning until afternoon, that 'poor
fellow' would sit crouched inside the quilt, reading or writing
something. No less than seven times would he ask for tea! There
are hundred other chores in the house. Who would attend to them
all?)

"Are you listening, *ji*, the water has already been heated
up. Why don't you get up and have your bath now? I can't keep
doing this 'bloody thing' all the time." Early in the morning at seven
o'clock, the wife had started ranting in her usual gruff manner.

'Who wants to shiver in such a cold weather, that too,
early in the morning on a holiday'. Thinking it over for awhile, he
spoke in a rather soft voice, "Why should I have an early bath?
Do I have to give away cows? Why don't you tell the girls to go in
for their bath?"

"Don't they have to go for their tuition?" Roared the wife
rather peevishly. "I've told you once that you'd better get up and
have your bath. Otherwise, you'll go around with an unwashed

face all day long. If you don't want it, I'm going to use up that
water for my bath."

He, too, lost his temper. What had happened to her early
in the morning? She was, no doubt, an ill-tempered person but
today her peevishness seemed to have crossed all limits.

When she came in to collect the empty teacups, he
twisted around to have a closer look at her face. The creases on
her forehead had deepened. He had never seen her looking so
peeved. It was a holiday and if that's the way they were going to
start their day, then how would it really end? Smiling his own
anger away, he grabbed hold of her arm, dragging her towards
the bed as she went breezing past him and said, "What kind of an
offering does *Kali Mai* expect today? – Why don't you come
and sit for a while? Let me persuade you to dissolve your anger a
little…!"

"Let it be!" With a sudden jerk she managed to release
her arm from his hold and the furrows on her forehead multiplied
manifold. Then as she went about putting away the bedding of the
three out of four beds that had somehow been squeezed into that
small, congested room, she kept muttering something all to herself.
"Yes, you can afford to talk… Is this a house? – You burn yourself
out all the time and yet no one appreciates a thing you do. Now
you'll keep lying here until the afternoon, with your topknot all
tied up; and then you'll quietly get up and go off somewhere.
Walk across to Chopra's house and play cards with him or drop
in at Garg's to have tea – all because if you have a glimpse of his
wife's *bindi* or hear her giggles, your day is well spent! Who the
hell is bothered about 'us'? You die several times during the day
or manage to live somehow…"

"Manage to live somehow" – that was it! As always, she
had got stuck on the same words that she repeated every time.
But whatever she had barked off earlier was rather strange. Never
before had she ever insinuated anything about Garg's wife. After
all, what had really happened to her today?

Shivering in the cold, he got off the bed, so that he could

help himself to hot water and start having his bath. But he could clearly hear the sounds of her mutterings inside as well. It did cross his mind that he, too, should shout her down but that would have only made the matters worse, not better. And it would have been pointless to aggravate the matters at this juncture when he ought to have facilitated them. Won't it dampen his holiday spirit? Such things were common on all other days but, at least, the holiday should be well spent.

The moment he came out after his bath, both the girls came in from his father's room and spoke in tandem, *"Bhapaji*, Masterji was asking for his tuition money."

"Money?" Running a comb through his hair, he turned around, surprised but seeing the face of his elder daughter, he was somewhat unnerved. He almost got a feeling as if there was a strange dread in the eyes of the girl – especially when she narrowed them down a little.

"He was saying, you must bring it today." The younger one, too, put her weight behind the words of the elder one.

A sudden spell of dizziness hit him, almost as if he was about to pass out. Dazed, he kept running the comb through his hair while repeatedly looking back at the younger one, who now stood head and shoulders above the elder one. Suddenly when he saw a feeling of reassurance dazzling in her light eyes, he broke into a smile.

"Money, I'll give you tomorrow – My little darling doesn't have to worry about money, does she?" As he gently tapped on her head with his knuckles, all three of them burst out laughing.

"*Nee*, may you burn all your hair. Are you now going for the tuition or not?" That very moment a piercing voice was heard from within the kitchen and both the girls slunk away, trembling in fear. But still the tirade of the wife had continued, unabated.

A sudden feeling of sadness descended upon him. He wasn't really in a mood to go anywhere. And it appeared ridiculous, retreating into the bed after the bath. He folded the bed, got in the wooden chair that was lying outside the kitchen and put it next to the table. And he sat down to read.

"What will I gain out of reading these law books?". A thought struck him all of a sudden. Putting the book away, he started drawing the image of a dog on a blank sheet of paper. That very moment, 'the queen of a wife' walked in, a broom in hand. She spoke rather brusquely, "Why don't you go out now? There's plenty of sunshine upon the rooftop. Then you'll say, I'm blowing dust in your face."

'Now she appears to be little better.' He thought to himself and quietly walked out of the room. On hearing that his father was being wracked by a bout of cough, he decided to peep into his room before going off towards the roof.

"*Pitaji*, have you had some tea?" Now that he had already entered the room, he just rolled off a question for the sake of saying something.

Pitaji first looked at him with fear-stricken eyes and then dragging in a deep breath, spoke in a sinking voice, "I'll get it."

He felt rage simmer deep inside. It was going to be half past eight or nine and so far no tea had been served to him. Seething with anger, as he went past the kitchen, he suddenly stopped on seeing tea with molasses boiling upon the hearth. His anger had now reached a flash point. That an asthmatic should be given tea mixed with molasses!... What does she think of herself? — But then it appeared as if he had heard the ear-shattering voice of his wife...

"Where should I go and burn this 'accursed' household! I get up at five in the morning and until midnight, I don't get a moment's respite. And still, it's you who have the upper hand! Tea mixed with molasses! – Go and get me *mishri*, I'll break it up and use it in tea! If you ask for sugar, all you get to hear is, '*Hai*, it costs money!'...I can't keep stoking the fires now. Am I made of iron or something?"

Without a word, he walked into the kitchen. Tears had welled up in his eyes, either because the smoke emanating from the hearth had hurt them or because his simmering anger had melted and started flowing through them.

Carrying the tea that he had poured into a bowl, which was covered as well, when he came back into the room, *Pitaji's* was in the middle of a racking bout of cough. For a long time he just kept sitting on the stool lying by his side. But when he finally handed over the tea, seeing the swollen and sagging flesh beneath his father's insomniac eyes and his wizened face and hands, a sudden feeling of sadness washed over him. While *Pitaji* had his tea, he just sat there looking around, dazed.

Not only were the edges of the bowl, which had ash in it and was lying between the wall and the bedpost, chipped but it also looked awfully dirty from outside. And the ash lay scattered upon the floor as well. A thick layer of dust had settled upon the bottle of glycodine that lay on the mantle piece. Next to it lay a bottle of medicine which having solidified in the manner of honey now looked quite unappealing. The girls had torn papers out of their rough copies and strewn them upon the tattered *durri*, spread out in one corner. As cement between the ridges of the bricks upon the floor had crumbled, it had left gaping holes, which now lay filled with dust. The whitewash, having flaked off the walls, now lay suffusing the floor. Close to the foundation, the wall had weakened because of the dampness. *Pitaji's* quilt was full of grime. And the pillow covers were equally dirty. No sheet had been spread on the mattress either. Even the muffler he had tied around his head was full of dirt.

And he began to feel nauseated. *Pitaji* wanted to discuss family matters with him but brushing him aside, he said, "You just sit outside for a while in the afternoon today. We'll clean up this room."

"What's wrong with its cleanliness? It's all right the way it is." *Pitaji* announced and then started asking him about the seven rupee raise he had been given.

But he had begun to feel suffocated. Making some excuse and picking up the bowl and the plate, he came out. Leaving the utensils in the kitchen and climbing up the stairs, he went straight to the roof. When he tried to read the book, nothing registered.

On picking up the newspaper, he was disgusted, seeing the grotesque picture of a few burnt up bodies of small children right on its front page. Staring at it blankly, he didn't feel like reading any news.

In the afternoon when the entire family sat down for the meals, he noticed that his wife hadn't had her bath yet. Grey hair next to her ears would fall over her face, time and again. While making the *rotis*, she would push them away very spontaneously but they would again fall over her face. The fire in the hearth had put itself out. As she sat blowing into it, trying to stoke it up, her eyes had turned blood-shot and the flesh underneath looked somewhat like mango *pappar* because she constantly rubbed that part with her *chunni*.

How did he think of this mango *pappar*? When he tried hard, his thoughts raced back to his childhood. For that is when he often used to buy it off the vendor outside the school for a few pennies. Licking it with his tongue, he would tear it off like a piece of leather, relishing every bit as he ate… Even the bag hanging off his shoulder now looked somewhat like mango *pappar* – partly because of the colour and partly because of the grime…He was first licking and sucking this mango *pappar* and then tearing it off like a piece of leather.

Suddenly a strange thought hit him. The *rotis* made of American wheat were also like the ones he was eating now. And he was tearing them off like mango *pappar* and eating – And perhaps that's how he had scraped the flesh off his wife, too…!

This expression 'scraping off' made him feel as though some vulture was pecking into a cadaver. A sudden feeling of disgust overwhelmed him. After downing a few gulps of water, he got up, leaving his meal unfinished. The wife didn't even bother to ask why he had not had his proper meal. When he returned to the room, a wave of nausea hit him again.

Spreading out the bed, he slipped back into the quilt, ostrich-like. He was about to drift into sleep but it simply winged away the moment he heard his wife talk to her daughters in so stern and brusque a manner as though they were her rivals. Picking up a book, he started thumbing through its pages rather casually. First he could spot a few words, then the words fell into a pattern but soon enough, he had drifted into a different world altogether...

What a strange world it was! The stars appeared to be in bloom almost like the flowers. Elf- like white women, their limbs moon-bathed, soaked in the fragrance of sandalwood and their feet henna-stained, were going to fill their pitchers of gold and silver from the ocean of sunlight...! Mesmerising eyes; long, wavy tresses; foreheads dazzling like the full-blown moon; elephantine gait and the dance of delicate feet, jingling with anklets – everything seemed as if it was happening right before his eyes.

"Put this comb away in the closet." The wife had dropped a bombshell into his magical world. Everything disappeared in a jiffy almost in the same way in which the shadows thin out from the surface of calm water the moment a pebble is cast into it.

He looked up. The wife was standing, bathed and dressed in a new suit. Now the deep furrows of her forehead or the tufts of grey hair behind her ears were not visible. She had applied a red lipstick as well. He felt like grabbing hold of her arm and dragging her towards the bed but he couldn't get to tear himself off the book completely. Picking up the comb, he put it on the table and went back to the book.

"*Hai, hai*, what a thing to do!" Bitterness had crept into wife's voice, again, "I said, you put it in the closet – and you've just thrown it away like that. As if we're never going to need it again?"

Now his concentration lay completely shattered. He had been made to lose his paradise for the sake of a worthless comb! The closet, too, was at such an awkward place, right next to his bedpost. Whenever anyone had to either take anything out from there or put it back, one had to go over his bed. So many times he had thought of shifting his bed elsewhere but it wasn't easy to arrange four beds in a 14x16 feet room. Even if he had managed to put the bed elsewhere, he wouldn't have been able to find a slot for his table overflowing with books.

He felt rather peeved. Picking up the comb, he threw it across into the closet with all his might. Rubbing her face with her hands, the wife stalked out of the room and now, raising the pitch of her voice, was busy arguing with the daughters, yet again.

He found himself in the throes of an inexplicable sadness. That moment, he just wanted to go off somewhere. Looking at the watch, he discovered that it was barely half past twelve. This was the time people usually had their meals on a holiday. So where should one go, really? It was a God forsaken moffusil town, much worse than a village. The moment you stepped out, heaps of garbage stared you in the face. There wasn't a single park, not even a regular road – all it had was a small distributary some two miles away. If you were to go and come back from there, the day would be put paid. Who had the leisure to go there?

He got up and started spring cleaning the closet. Picking up several useless papers, old letters, empty bottles, one broken mirror and a few plastic casements, he threw them all away in the dustbin. He arranged the books, once again, in the upper shelf. In the lower one, he put away the mirror, combs, the oil bottle, empty cream bottle and other odds and ends in an orderly manner. And he dumped all the useless stuff that was lying in the lower most shelf in one corner of the kitchen. Coming back into the room as he glanced at the closet, again, this time it really appealed to his eyes. Then he set about arranging the trunk, the beds, utensils and a few other small things. The wife, too, lent him a helping hand.

He looked at the watch. It was going to be half past four. "At least, the day is over! The holiday has passed off!"

He dusted his clothes, washed his face and made himself a cup of tea. Calling the girls down from the roof, he gave them tea as well. He talked to them about their studies and shared a few wisecracks about their teachers. Picking up the bag when he was about to leave for the market, he felt much lighter.

Going past *Pitaji's* room, he just happened to ask, casually,

"*Pitaji*, you want me to bring you something to eat from the bazaar?" All he did was nod dissent. At least, he did his duty! Now he was feeling all the more lighter.

After enjoying tea and gossip with two of his friends when he returned, the bag full of vegetables dangling across his shoulder, he met up with Hardev Singh outside the gate itself. When he tried to drag him inside for some tea and snacks, Hardev refused, pulling a long face.

"You please take these sugarcane sticks and *saag* along…I've come to seek your forgiveness!" With these words, Hardev cast his eyes downwards, almost like a criminal.

He was rather surprised. Then he learnt that the dog had died of pneumonia the previous night. When he learnt about it, he laughed and said, "I was wondering what has happened? It's only a dog, not an elephant, which has died, after all? – So what if he died, it's all right."

Carrying the sugarcane sticks and *saag* as he came inside, satisfaction was writ large on his face. Off-loading the pile of sugarcane sticks outside the kitchen, he broke the news of the dog's death to his wife in a rather cavalier manner. Looking totally shocked, she started knocking her hands upon her knees.

"*Hai*, this misfortune upon my head! What's this? They must have poisoned our poor Tanny!" As the wife dragged in a deep breath, her voice nearly trembled and eyes misted over.

Standing there, he kept looking at the yellow stain of turmeric her hand had left on her new *latha salwar.* 'The turmeric stain doesn't go at all…it turns red when you try to wash the cloth' – This thought hit him, time and again.

The wife had actually been reduced to tears. She had started sniffling as well. On hearing the sound, even the girls came and stood outside the kitchen. When they learnt about the real thing, they, too, became rather emotional. Strangely enough, death of the dog didn't appear unusual to him at all. Rather he felt as though he always knew that they were going to get rid of the dog soon. (So many times they had fought over whether or not to keep the dog. 'When they themselves were worried about the food, what were they going to do with the dog, bang their heads against him?' But the wife simply refused to listen to him. She would often say – 'How much of your food does he eat, after all?' Not just three *rotis* in the morning and three in the evening, but also *daal*, vegetables, a quarter kilo of milk and *lassi* to top it all. He ate as much as any ordinary adult would. And yet she would say, 'How much of your food does he eat, after all?')

Quietly, he came in. He was breathing very freely now. After removing his shoes, he lay down upon the *manji*.

While cooking the meals and settling the utensils, the wife kept muttering all to herself. Who knows what kind of abuses she kept mumbling against Hardev Singh. And then while washing the dishes she suddenly barged into the room, as if merely to show him the leavings of *rotis,* mixed with a thick gruel of *daal* and water. Coming closer to his bed, she said, "Isn't this the kind of stuff he always ate? Or did you ever feed him *pedas?*" Stepping forward, she emptied out the dirty gruel upon the floor, next to a small drain. And then she went back to washing dishes in the kitchen, muttering under her breath all this while.

'Now what does this mean?' He thought to himself. 'What did I say to her that she is getting so uptight with me?' Though he wasn't able to figure anything out, he felt strangely relieved. It was almost as if he had begun to relish the taste of his wife's bitter words. So pricking his ears, he started listening to her words carefully. She was repeating the same thing over and over again, "Here, can I call anyone my own? Can I really? He goes off to the office and children to the school – and I stay here condemned! But who bothers? After all, one has to spend the day somehow."

Tired of this useless blabber, he returned to the same book he was reading in the afternoon.

    *   *   *

For three days, thereafter, the wife just kept harping on the same thing about the dog. Whatever be the point of discussion, she would somehow manoeuvre to drag the dog into the conversation. Things like, "Had he been around, could the crow have dared to put its beak into *daal*?" And then in the evening, her hand resting upon her chest, she would take a deep sigh and say, "Really, my heart sinks the moment I think of him – I was so attached to him!"

Now this bit about being 'attached' was rather strange. Did she mean to say that the woman who was more of a *Kalka Mai* than a mother to her own children and who was always ready to pounce upon her husband could possibly have loved cats and dogs? Without saying a word, he just kept smiling all to himself, his eyes downcast.

That very night, around mid-night *Pitaji* had a sudden attack and passed away. On hearing the news, several neighbours came rushing in. When he first ran across to call the doctor over, he didn't feel anything; when *Pitaji* passed away, still he didn't feel anything; even when he poured *Gangajal* into his mouth, he didn't feel anything; but when the people started assembling, he broke into heart-rending wails and cries. Freeing himself from their hold, he started hitting his head against the walls. Pundit Prem Sagar did try to calm him down, but his tears just wouldn't stop. Finally, it was Master Ram Prasad who gave voice to his heart-felt emotions when he said, "*Punditji*, this is what the web of attachment is all about! It's something beyond the control of all human beings!"

But once *Pitaji's kirya* ceremony was over and a discussion about his good qualities had started among the people, he felt as if a great burden had dropped away from his mind. When Pundit Prem Sagar started *expatiating on* the kind of responsibilities this 'turban' entailed, he made quick calculations about the money lying at home. That gave him much greater relief. He would manage and the need to borrow more money wouldn't simply arise. Even if he has to, he'll be able to pay it back soon – now it would mean less expenses as they were two less!

Thinking about this reduced expenditure, he twisted around

to see if anyone had read his thoughts. It was a sheer illusion; no one had noticed either him or his thoughts.

That very evening, as the wife went into *Pitaji's* room, a broom in her hand, she said, "Let me settle the room now. It looks bad when the guests drop by. Of course, the whitewash can wait until after *Dussehra.*"

He felt a little better now. It was as if it hadn't occurred to him until then that now they had two rooms. How can you really manage without two rooms these days? You do need an extra room for the guests who just might come along.

The Dam

Resting his hand upon the wooden bar of the hoe as Pakhar looked up, the rows of people approaching appeared to him to be somewhat like swarms of bees. Surprised, he peeled his eyes hard to see in the dark but could barely spot anything very clearly. (Sleeplessness and exhaustion of the past three days had strained his body, but he was still busy working hard in trying to strengthen the banks of the dam. Being tired and hungry, he found it hard to dig in his hoe even as far as his feet.)

Now all those people were crossing over the peak of the dam. Ever since Pakhar had started observing them, all he had been able to see clearly was the man walking ahead of them. He was sporting a starched, white turban, loose-sleeved *kurta,* and a tight-fitting pajama. He looked quite gentlemanly and God-fearing. Behind his crystal clear specks, his eyes lay smiling. As he walked apace, he sometimes glanced at the rising table of the swirling waters overrunning the banks of the dam, and sometimes at the people working overtime on the other side, shovelling the earth in an effort to plug the breach.

For quite some time, Pakhar kept staring at him. Though he had seen the face already, it was not easy to recognise him. Then he ran his gaze towards the people who were bringing up the rear. Now everything had begun to fall in place for him. All these people were apparently from the city. Newly washed, white clothes, and oil-soaked hair styled in perfection. Some of them were even laughing and joking about the rising waters; others were enjoying the spectacle of the water spreading all around, but some of them had their foreheads creased as they looked at the water rather anxiously, wondering how and when the rage of the swirling waters would ultimately subside. Occasionally, they would let a deep sigh escape their lips, as if saying "Oh-ho" or "*Bhagwan* has really done a bad thing." It wasn't so much the presence of those enjoying this spectacle or laughing and joking with each other that irritated Pakhar, as did the hysterical reactions of those who seemed to be going through the motions of practised behaviour. For some reason, he felt as though they were jeering at his *bapu's* white, straggly beard.

The city folks would first march right up to the far end of the dam, and then return. Pakhar felt as though they were mere spectators, out for fun. And looking at them, he felt no different. But the moment such a thought hit him, he would instantly turn his attention away from them, and start digging in and shovelling the soil.

After a while, he heard a familiar voice from somewhere close to the dam. He looked up, again. The same man with a starched turban and the village *sarpanch* were coming in, talking to each other. Looking around rather furtively, the man with a starched turban was talking in a very secretive albeit meaningful manner. Though Pakhar could hardly understand anything of what he said, he did manage to hear the word 'vote,' which that fellow used repeatedly. And slowly, the identity of that fellow had begun to dawn upon him as well.

He was the same person who had come to assist the sarpanch when 'votes' were to be cast for the village panchayat. Almost everyone in the village knew that he had given a good deal of money to his 'henchmen' to buy off the votes. They had offered, no, not the bottles, rather several caskets of liquor to the ill-reputed characters. Using all the means, fair or foul, he had garnered a fifteen-twenty vote win for the sarpanch owing allegiance to his group. It hadn't taken people more than a couple of months to realise that they were in for trouble. Those who had cast their votes in return for five or ten rupees now found it difficult to go even as far as the outer boundary of the village. More than half of the land along the boundary was now in the possession of the sarpanch and his musclemen had absolutely no qualms about teasing anyone's daughter or sister. Even if someone as much as dared to break a twig for a *datun*, they would start fighting with him. In the past couple of months, they had beaten a good number of labourers to pulp. But during the assembly elections, when the same fellow started doing the rounds of the village along with the sarpanch, canvassing for his party, the entire village had held a meeting and made it known to him quite explicitly that this time round they wouldn't be able to go along with him. He had returned without a word, and the people had refused to vote for him. It was only now when this calamity struck did the people wake up to the fact how he had harboured that grudge all along. Since the floods had hit, it was being said that two motor boats for rescuing people had been put into operation in the adjoining village. But not even a single one had been sent to Pakhar's village. It was also being said that this very man with a starched turban was the one responsible for requisitioning the boats. He enjoyed a great deal of respect and prestige in the government circles, even among the administrators. If he wanted, he could have sent the rescue boats to Pakhar's village as well, but it was sheer vindictiveness that had prevented him from doing so. Sarpanch was the one who had communicated this to the people. And he was also saying that even now if they were to go and put their turbans at his feet, begging for help, he would be ready to arrange for every possible help. "He's a God-fearing man and it really wouldn't take much to please him." But so far people had refused to heed the sarpanch's advice. Some of them had taken such an exception to his suggestion of putting the turbans at his feet that they had started fighting with him.

But today, that fellow had come to them on his own. For a while, at least, Pakhar felt as though he really was a God-fearing soul, but the next moment when he glanced up at the city-folks walking on the banks of the dam, he felt that they were in no way different from him. (Rather that man with a starched turban appeared to be their gang-leader). He felt a burning sensation in the pupils of his eyes. Once again, he started shovelling the earth in a hurry. But his heart was becoming more and more restive.

The sun was about to go down. The reflection of its crimson light shimmering upon the surface of water appeared rather splendid. In this shimmering light, the city folks shone somewhat like the cranes. Rooted to the ground, Pakhar just kept staring at them, fixedly. Accompanied by the sarpanch, that fellow had now walked up to the railway track. After shaking hands with the sarpanch, that fellow rode his motorbike and sped off. Other city-folks followed him on their bicycles, and some had even started walking along the railway track. Right behind the track, close to the pond, as the sun had already set these people and other city-folks appeared to Pakhar to be no more than the moving shadows of the ghosts. First he felt somewhat scared of these shadows but then his head became rather feverish. With all his might, he first cut his hoe rather deeply into the soil, and then heaving up a loadful of earth, threw it towards the dam, his face puckering up into a scowl. Then hitting the wet earth with the other end of the hoe, he solidified it over the dam. This did calm down Pakhar's restive mind a little as though the dam had finally been fortified now....

Once again, Pakhar looked towards the railway track and then with the view to rest awhile, he clambered over the other side of the dam. Now he could not only see the shadowy figures of the city-folks but also see people from his own village, who sat helplessly under a blue tent, pitched upon a high mound. Looking towards the wailing children lying under the makeshift hutments of manjis and carts, and the soot-laden faces of the women who used wet firewood, Pakhar felt as though he had either come to a strange land or was seeing a nightmare. He felt as if this high mound was some kind of a tall bush in the middle of vast expanse of water, and the occasional clouds of smoke rising, no different from the smoked-out edges of the bush. And somewhere among these burnt-out edges of the bushes were hiding his five children, wife and old father, though no one had so far come forward to help them... These city-folks had mainly come to see the spectacle of the floodwaters rising...

Peeling his eyes rather hard and his forehead creased, Pakhar looked in the direction of the railway track, once again. The shadows of the city-folks had deepened a little, and now they had begun to appear rather revolting to him.

(The first time, Pakhar had felt revolted by these city-folks when Kundan Shah had come from town, armed with a law decree for the attachment of his father's property. When Pakhar was still a child, at the end of every harvest season, Kundan Shah would visit their house. And each time he would leave only after he had managed to get Pakhar's thumb impression as well upon his account books. That time, Pakhar didn't find him so repulsive. But when he came along with the court officials and simply took away their buffalo and both the bulls, the cart and even the heifer that Pakhar had reared, then he had felt like giving him a crushing blow on his head with other end of his hoe, though being much younger in age, he had felt rather helpless. From that day onwards, he had begun to nurse a deep-seated hatred for the city-folks, and every city-based person appeared to him to be no different from Kundan Shah.).

(Once he had grown up into a young man, he heard all kinds of strange stories about the city-folks from his close friend, Jaggu. About their huge, palatial havelis, once Jaggu had told him that these were often bought out of their 'ill-begotten money.' As a matter of fact, most of the city-based persons who would often be seen lounging around in their shops, reclining against huge pillows, had amassed all their 'ill-begotten wealth' by exploiting the jats and it was this 'ill-earned wealth' that had made the likes of them as affluent as Kundan Shah. No wonder, ever since his childhood, hatred for such Kundan Shahs had struck deep roots in his heart. Although Pakhar did know that many of the city-folks were not only poor but also had wiry, shapeless bodies, especially those who simply sat at the shop all through the day, weighing grams and flour, yet his hatred for the city-folks was not lessened in any way. The fact of the matter was that he found the very mention of the word 'city-folks' hateful).

As he sat on top of the dam, lost in his own thoughts, Pakhar Singh would sometimes look at the railway track and sometimes, at his waterlogged land. Slowly, the darkness was closing in upon him. Though the shadows of the city-folks were no longer visible, somehow their contours were still dancing in front of Pakhar's eyes.

"What if this dam were to be washed away...!" The moment this thought struck Pakhar, he felt as though the dam had slowly begun to dissolve, just like a heap of sand and that the swirling waters had flooded the land right up to the railway track, drowning everything under its mighty sweep... Within minutes, the water had entered the streets of the town... flooding in the pucca houses as well... and the city-folks, desperately crying for help, had started running to safer places... all of them included, that man with a starched turban and Kundan Shah... Their faces had turned ashen pale... As right in front of their eyes, the very foundations of their havelis, built out of the 'ill-begotten money' were splittting up... huge pillows and mattresses were being swept away... and the wads of notes lying in their cash boxes were floating on the surface of water, just like the cotton balls... and this is how the 'ill-begotten wealth' was being swept away...

"Pakhar, bai, here's some roti for you," Ghudda, the panch spoke up as he came up from behind.

Startled, Pakhar looked back, and then after wiping his hands off his kurta, he took the rotis from him.

"Now you'd better watch out. We put you on this duty only because you're strong and wise. The water level is rising slowly. So just take care that all this effort of the past three days or so doesn't go waste," said the panch, while leaving.

It appeared as though Pakhar hadn't heard a word. Even now, it was the same image dancing before his eyes, havelis of the city folks collapsing amidst the swirling floodwaters. When he put the first morsel in his mouth, it suddenly struck him that he was smiling all to himself. Without so much as being conscious of it, he had already dug a few inches deep tunnel under the mud-dyke, hacking away at the earth slowly with the edge of his hoe. While chewing the morsel when his eyes suddenly fell upon this tunnel, he was rather surprised. After he had given it some thought, a sudden smile suffused his face as he stared at the tunnel that appeared more like a snake stretching out in the dark. While eating his meal, all kinds of strange thoughts came crowding into Pakhar's mind. But suddenly when he heard some commotion rise from the direction of the railway track, his attention was drawn away. As it was pitch dark, he couldn't see anything much ahead. But it didn't take him long to realise that after wading though neck-deep water, the city-folks were advancing towards the high mound, balancing the baskets full of rotis upon their heads.

'City-folks!' It was as if this expression hit Pakhar's whole being with the force of a hammer. He wondered how these people, who were wading through neck-deep waters, mornings and evenings, so as to be able to feed the youngsters working on the fortification of the dam, and who were toiling day and night to provide food to their children, could be the same city-folks? …And it was as if the blinkers had slipped off his eyes: every inhabitant of a city is not a city-folk. These people also live in the city. But their clothes were grimier and more tattered than those of Pakhar. There was hardly any flesh upon their bones. Yesterday, one of them was telling him that most of them lived in the bastis, on the outskirts of the city. …'And those bastis, God forbid, even an enemy should never have to reside in them.' Pakhar thought all to himself. In these bastis, there were small tenements, more sordid and narrower than his old hutment. In the narrow, congested streets, slush and garbage could be seen everywhere around. One day, when Pakhar was going past the cotton factory, seeing such a basti, he had been reminded of an old saw, 'Hell must be just like this.' And on seeing those people, Pakhar had felt a sudden wave of compassion surge inside).

'Then how could these people be city-folks? …They

couldn't possibly be living off their 'ill-begotten money' — It appeared as though hunger had shrunk their livers, too....' Pakhar was thinking all to himself.

Then shovelling the earth with his feet, he plugged the tunnel dug up earlier with his hoe.

Darkness had descended all around. The swishing of the swirling waters, the constant buzz of the hoes digging into the earth, the youngsters piling heap upon heap of earth towards the far end of the dam and the children wailing upon the mound; all these sounds appeared to cut through the stillness of the night. Although Pakhar felt starved, his self-absorption had slowed down his eating so much that until then he had barely managed to finish two of his rotis. While chewing each morsel, he would suddenly be reminded of those people living in the bastis who had either been cooking or collecting rotis for them for the past three days....
'Oye, the dam has burst, the dam has finally burst...'

Pakhar first heard this tremulous voice coming up from behind and then, a medley of voices, rising to a crescendo, 'Dam has collapsed.' Then he felt as though it was the sound of their hurried footfalls that made the ground tremble beneath their feet. Startled, he stood up, though he hadn't been able to take to his heels.

Pakhar looked towards his right, and indeed, it was an amazing sight. The lights flickering upon the city made him feel that the dawn was almost about to split. As he smiled all to himself, it appeared to him that commotion of the people was akin to what the city-folks would create 'a few *hours later,*' once the rising floodwaters, now flowing only up to the level of the railway track, would go swirling through their houses, washing away their thresholds... When their 'ill-begotten wealth' would be...

But suddenly when Pakhar's eyes fell upon the half-eaten roti spread out on his palm, a giddy sensation gripped him... The people who brought in these rotis were also from a basti in one of the low-lying areas close to the railway track and so, first of all, the water would....

"Oh!" This was about all that escaped Pakhar's lips. Tucking rest of the roti into his turban, he ran desperately towards that direction from where the voices were coming.

Silent Rage

As he neared the small dusty track leading up to the village, Bhunda, the dumb one, happened to pull the wedge off the plough, bringing the bullocks to an abrupt halt. Narrowing his eyes, he ran his gaze far across the pathway. Along the corner of the pathway, he spotted a woman walking down the track, balancing *rotis* upon her head. When he looked hard enough, he saw that it was none other than Jalo, the daughter of Namha *majhabi*.

"Uh—hoo-hoo-hoo!" The dumb one laughed. For some time, he just stood there, laughing and narrowing his eyes by turns.

Now Jalo was only a field away from him. Making a clumsy sound signalling the bullocks to stay put, the dumb one set off towards the dusty track. Dusting off his dust-smeared, *khaddar* headgear by cracking up his hands on both sides of his head, he went bounding across and positioned himself in the middle of the track. With his legs wide apart, his hands upon his thighs and his neck stiff as ramrod, he stood there in the manner of a heifer, all set to accost Jalo .She, too, had seen him and perhaps being a little scared of him, she had started walking towards the edge of the track, close to the fence. Her slow gait had not faltered, though.

She was about ten steps away from him, when the dumb one hollered "Uh-baa" and his eyes nearly popped out in surprise. Jalo was coming along, wiping her eyes with the *chunni*. Running towards her, the dumb one got hold of her arm without the least trace of hesitation, and started dragging her towards the fields, doing "Uh-baa, Uh-baa" all this while. First Jalo did resist a little, but then she started following him up. Even now her gait showed no signs of a hasty stagger. Dragging her across to the tree and swiftly removing the *rotis* and the jug full of *lassi* off her head, the dumb one pulled her hand down, gesturing her to sit on the ground. With her tear-stained, swollen, red eyes, Jalo started staring around rather helplessly, first towards the dusty track and then at the fields that lay sprawling in the front. The dumb one understood immediately. Having looked around carefully, he started rotating his hand like a drum, close to her face, repeating "Uh-baa" each time to reassure her that there was no one in the vicinity.

It was in his rough hands that the dumb one was holding Jalo's arm, wide as the dove's neck. When he gave it another jerk to make her sit down, tears brimming in Jalo's eyelids, started to roll off, falling upon the dumb one's thick, hairy hands. When she sat down rather disinterestedly, wiping her tears with her *chunni*, she hid her entire face with it.

"Uh-baa-haa!" Raising his hand close to Jalo's face, he gestured as though he was asking her, "What's this, Jalo? Why are you ruining such beautiful eyes with your saline tears?"

But Jalo had started howling all the more loudly. Wracked by her sobs, her soft, supple body was trembling all over. First, his grip loosened over Jalo's arm ever so slowly, and then, he let go of it completely. His fingers, hard as the blade of pincers, had become softer than a tangled skein of roots. Jalo's sobs appeared to be cutting through his skin, squeezing life out of his demon-sized body. Momentarily, he stood there, staring at Jalo from head to toe. Then, shouting "Uh-baa-baa-haa" in his squeaky voice, he pulled at her *chunni* to draw her attention and folded up both his hands in a gesture of extreme helplessness. Even his eyes had such a pleading look in them that they could have easily melted a stone of heart, too. Such expressions had appeared on his coarse, thickset face that it almost looked like a squeezed-out honeycomb. Jalo had not removed the *chunni* off her face but she could read all the expressions of the dumb one from the way in which he was making abortive bids to express himself. Each time he touched her arm, knee or forehead momentarily, saying "Uh—baa-haa" in his squeaky drawl, Jalo could feel the tremor of his silent, dumb pleas race through her body. Overshadowing the painful memory of that incident that had occurred near the threshing floor, his pleas appeared to bring a strange comfort to her distraught mind. After wiping her tears when Jalo looked up, seeing a rare suppleness on his coarse, simple face, she could not believe that it was the face of the same Bhunda.

"Uh-baa-ha-ha..." Hollering again in his pronounced drawl, the dumb one bent over to touch his forehead to the ground as though he were paying obeisance to Jalo and pleading desperately, "Come on, out with it, now?"

And this time as the dumb one lifted his head to peer into Jalo's eyes, she was unable to endure his look. (Who knows whether or not any Majnu had ever looked at his Laila in this manner; or Mirza, his Sahiban; or Ranjha, his Heer...Was it possible for them to verbalise all those secrets of the heart that now spoke through the transparent eyes of the dumb one). Though Jalo felt a strange tremor run through her entire body, yet she could not take her wet eyes off the dumb one's; but when she finally did it was as though she was gorging her own eyes out. It was strange how she had felt a sudden stab of a pain while taking her eyes off, something that had made them limpid all over again.

"Hoon-uh-uh-aah!" Whispering this very softly, the dumb one lowered his eyes. A strange dread had appeared on his face, the ominous dread of the unknown.

But when the dumb one looked up, again, the same raggedness had returned to his face. Again, grabbing hold of Jalo's arm with his coarse fingers, he started shaking her, repeating the refrain of "Uh-baa," "Uh-baa." He was asking her very firmly, "Hurry up and tell me, what's happened?"

Very hesitantly, Jalo gestured towards the threshing floor and then pointing towards the arm that the dumb one was holding, she explained how someone had grabbed hold of her arm in this very manner.

Shouting "Uh-baa" "Uh-baa" the dumb one opened his eyes so wide as though his eyes would instantly gobble up that person who had dared to hold her arm.

In a bid to extract more information about that person, Bhunda had started shaking her arm repeatedly, but Jalo sat there unmoved, her eyes lowered. Her eyes had begun to brim over. For a while he sat down, his back resting against the tree as though he was busy reflecting over something. Then repeating the incoherent sounds of "Uh-Uh," he lifted Jalo's chin a little to draw her attention towards himself and started gesturing rather frantically to know who it was. First he ballooned his cheeks, then twirling his moustaches, he glared as though he were asking, "Is he the same person who keeps twirling his moustaches all the time and who has his cheeks always bulging out?" When Jalo nodded her head in affirmation, Bhunda stood up on his feet to seek confirmation of his worst fears. He stood with his legs wide apart, just the way *zaildar's kaka* would always stand on the threshold of his *baithak*, his *chaddar* pulled up to his knees. Besides, he twirled his moustaches and did "Uh-baa," even tried to bring in the same expression which *kaka's* drunken eyes always had as he leered at the daughters and daughters-in-law of the village, walking down his street. Then he leapt across to Jalo, sat down beside her and shaking his head vigorously, repeating "Uh-baa-haa" each time, he started asking her, "Was it really *zaildar's kaka* who held her arm?"

Jalo had the satisfaction now that the dumb one had understood everything. While nodding her head in affirmation, she could almost feel the pain of *kaka's* tenacious grip on her arm and the ferocity of his drunken eyes with which he had looked at her. She could even hear the menacing words he had spoken as she had jerked her arm out of his grip, "You think of yourself as some fairy or something! If we get it into our head, we'll pull this thorn out by the evening. Do you understand! In this inebriated state, you just might mistake cotton for the curd and end up eating it." Momentarily, a sudden rage flashed in Jalo's eyes. But the moment, she was reminded of his threatening words, "So, you'd better wait until the evening and see what *tamasha* we do," her entire body trembled in fear and eyes brimmed over, again.

"Uh-hee!" With a piercing shriek, the dumb one suddenly bounced upon his feet and stood up.

Jalo was petrified. Wiping her tears off as she looked at the dumb one, her heart suddenly started pounding with some unknown fear. Such a dreadful face she had not even seen in her dreams ever. Only a moment ago, honey seemed to be dripping off each feature of the dumb one's face, but now it seemed as though it had been cast in stone. His pupils were bulging out in such a frightful manner as though his eyes had virtually split. Rooted to the ground, like the banyan tree near the village pond, he was staring towards the village in such a manner as though he wanted to burn down all the *kothas, kaccha* as well as *puccha.*

Jalo could not bear to look at him any longer. Picking the jug of *lassi* and the *rotis* off the ground with her trembling hands, she stood up. While leaving, she raised her finger towards the dumb one's face and told him in a quavering voice, "Now, you'd better be careful. Don't you create any enmity for my sake! ...Oh, I'm the accursed one! Had it not been so, wouldn't God have given me a brother. He would have, at least, saved me from the claws of such butchers..."

With these words Jalo left, her eyes still flushed with tears, disregarding that in his present state, the dumb one could neither listen to her words nor heed her advice. Standing like a ramrod and staring wildly towards the village, his neck as stiff as that of a heifer, the dumb one had kept twirling his moustaches for a long time. (Now he could not see anything apart from the new *chaubaras* of the *zaildar* flashing before his eyes as they rose above the *kaccha kothas.*)

"Uh-baa-ah-haa...!" Hollering once again, the dumb one dug his teeth so deep into his left hand that its impact remained visible for a long time.

Jumping across the dusty track over to the small pathway

running through the fields as Jalo heard his scream, her trembling heart started pounding all the more heavily. Momentarily, she turned back to glance at him but the very next moment, she had pressed on ahead, fear trailing her each step.

The dumb one was still standing there under the tree, like a log of *keekar*. The image of *zaildar's kaka* would suddenly flash before his eyes and then dissolve again. He had a fair idea of all his despicable deeds. Earlier too, the dumb one had felt enraged at his deeds, but never so much as he did now. Almost in a flash, his misdeeds came back to the dumb one.

For the past two years, this elder son of *zaildar* (who was called *kaka* although he was close to thirty now) had really created a furore in the village. He would sit in his *baithak*, drink and play cards with his roughnecks, and keep doing "hah-hah" "hi-hi" all through the day. Whenever he so fancied, he would come and stand outside on the threshold of his *baithak*, start twirling his moustaches and openly leer at the daughters and sisters walking past the street. When dead-drunk, he would start talking nonsense as well. (Being dead scared of him, no one ever challenged him. Last year, when two loafers decided to throw him a gauntlet, they had been taught quite a lesson. He had dumped illegal arms in their house and later had them arrested. Both of them were still in jail. Some people thought that the real cause of *kaka's* heady power-mania was that the candidate he had supported in the previous elections now occupied an important position somewhere. It was on the strength of his proximity to that man that he often took all kinds of liberties with everyone and everything. Even the junior officers of the area had a fair idea of his powerful connections and so were scared of him).

Since last year, he had been chasing Jalo around. Whenever he had a chance encounter with her, he would accost poor Jalo. Seeing Jalo petrified, shrinking away in a desperate bid to slip off, he would often burst into a demonic laughter such as only a hunter laughs when he sees a bird trapped in his net, struggling to make an unsuccessful bid to flee. (And whose neck he could twist any time he wanted). At all odd hours, he would go visiting Jalo's house as well. Twirling his moustaches, he would often call out from outside, "Is *Sardar Bahadur* home?" And then smiling all to himself, he would leave as suddenly as he came. In such moments of fear, crouching close to the bolted door, Jalo often felt her rage reach a flash point. What made it unbearable for Jalo was the manner in which he often chewed the expression '*Sardar Bahadur*' between his teeth as he spoke. That moment, she just wanted to pick up an axe and bring it down upon his neck. But then, thinking about *kaka's* 'status,' she would simply burst into tears and lighten her burden.

Last year, when Jalo's father was working as a *siri* along with the dumb one and several others, it did occur to her that she should disclose it to the dumb one. Then she would think to herself, "How is the dumb one related to me?" And this was something she hadn't quite understood as to what kind of relationship she had with the dumb one.

In those days of the *siri,* when she either went to the house of the dumb one to work or help him out in the fields, he would break into a smile the moment he saw her. Initially, seeing the dumb one smile in this manner, she used to feel rather scared. But slowly her fear melted away as she saw that he did nothing more than flash a smile at her, even when she met him alone sometimes. As on several occasions, the dumb one simply came forward to help her offload the baskets full of dung-heap or slice off the fodder and carry it away or offer to carry the *roti* to the fields himself, Jalo had begun to like him somewhat. Occasionally, when he looked straight into her eyes, becoming self-conscious, she would lower her eyes instantly. The dumb one would do "ha-ha-hanh" and burst into a loud laughter, even hold her hand and press it sometimes but then let go of it the very next moment. His expressionless eyes would then fail to meet Jalo's gaze for days on end, though the crimson shade of Jalo's embarrassment could be seen pasted on his rugged features for a long time thereafter. Such were the moments when Jalo simply wanted to grab hold of his coarse-grained, hairy arm and bend him towards herself. But this was something she had not been able to will herself to do.

Slowly, the dumb one became the axis of Jalo's life, as it were. The young daughter of a blind mother and a feeble father, Jalo now regarded herself secure because of the dumb one. (Many a time, she had been able to face the village hoodlums on the strength of this very knowledge and seeing her indomitable courage, they, too, had retreated. But when confronted by *kaka*, she had found herself to be completely helpless. She could neither say anything to him nor tell the dumb one about it. Little did she know that twice or thrice, the dumb one had seen with his own eyes how *kaka* had accosted her).

Jalo turned back, once again. The dumb one was still standing there. Then lowering her eyes, she set off towards the pathway, staring at the dust rising off the track. She had failed to notice that after digging teeth into his hand and shrieking again, the dumb one had gone bounding back to his plough.

Seeing him rush in towards them in this manner, the bullocks, too, had begun to tremble. Two bouncing leaps and he had grabbed hold of their horns and in the batting of an eyelid, he had removed the yoke off their necks. Slapping their backs rather hard, he sent them bounding towards the tree. Then putting his feet firmly upon the wooden support of the plough, he gave it such a jerk with his one hand that it split into two, so easily as though it were no more than a slender stick. Heaving the chopped up support of the plough upon his shoulder, the dumb one again stood there just the way he had under the tree, a while ago. Narrowing his blood-shot eyes, as red as flaming embers, he darted another glance at the *zaildar's chaubara* and as he did so, his eyes nearly popped out.

"Uh-baa-baa-haa-haa…!" Biting into his hand once again, he stamped his right foot upon the ground with such force that the moment it fell under his heel, a sod as hard as a rock crumbled like a *ladoo* of boiled rice.

Then bending his head, he rushed towards the open fields

that lay ahead. He kept running as wildly until he had reached the dusty track. Such was the demonic expression in his fiery eyes as if he wanted to reduce the entire earth to a pile of ashes. The moment he reached the dusty track, he stopped abruptly. "Khooh!" nasalising a menacing sound he first stopped and then hollered "Uh-baa-haa," once again, with such disgust that his whole body began to tremble.

With his neck stiff as ramrod, his grindstone-like chest swelling out and his legs wide apart, he had started walking ever so slowly, as though he were some wrestler heading towards the *akhara* for a bout. Right up to the village, he had continued to walk in that very manner. (His eyes were constantly riveted upon *zaildar's chaubara*.) On entering the interior track, he looked straight at their street and then suddenly stopped in the middle.

Kaka was standing upon the threshold of his *baithak*, a gold-embroidered *jutti* in his feet. Around his neck hung a milk-white, loose *kurta* of muslin and around his waist a piece of cloth lay wrapped. Lifting up that piece of cloth with his left hand, he was busy twirling his moustaches with his right. Seated inside, five or six of his roughnecks were busy creating ruckus as they played cards.

The moment, the dumb one saw the edge of *kaka's kurta,* he clenched his teeth and hollered "Uh-baa-baa-baa-baa-hi-uh…!" with such ferocity that his own hands nearly pulled out the hair of his moustaches he was tugging at.

Then he ran frantically towards *kaka,* his head bent low. When the children playing in the street saw him rush headlong in this manner, they immediately hustled off and stood waiting, their backs up against the street-walls.

Black Bull

"Oye Debeya, get some *lassi* from there." Attra called out to his young nephew. "You think, there's a pond full of *lassi* here." Rather than Deba, it was Attra's *bharjai* Shamo who had replied, "You behave as if you haven't ever seen anything. God alone knows why all the God-forsaken lepers have had to throng here!" Then for a long time thereafter, she had kept mumbling all to herself.

Embarrassed, Attra got up. He had never raised his voice in Shamo's presence.

She was the one who had practically brought him up like her own children. He was barely ten when his mother died and then it was Shamo who looked after him.

Quietly, he put the spade on his shoulder and left for the fields. He was feeling rather sad, though.

A little distance away from Kartara's *kothri,* he met Bacchni who had a basket upon her head. His sadness was suddenly halved. He picked up his stride to join in with her. By the time he had reached by her side, she had begun to pull the dung-cakes out of the pile. Inching closer to the *kothri,* Attra slowed down a little, then looking around, he picked up a sod and threw it, targetting Bacchni's back, apparently in a bid to tease her. She turned around and started smiling.

"Should I carry the basket for you? You'll be bothered,

without a reason," said Attra with a laugh.

"*Weh*, do you want to eat these up with a caper fruit? Your knees start bending the moment you cross the dyke. And you'll carry the basket?" Bacchni retorted, sarcasm showing through.

"I don't know. It appears, you have to lug around quite a few wooden beams for using up as firewood."

Looking around stealthily when Attra saw that there was no one lurking, he jumped across to where she was sitting.

"I don't know about the beams. But I'm certainly stronger than you." Bacchni challenged his manhood and he felt rather sheepish.

"Yes, why not? Haven't you suckled the brown-coloured buffaloes?" He could not think of a more innocent reply than this.

"I don't keep drowning myself in *lassi* all the time."

"As if you possess a cow who gives forty kilos of milk! That dry-skinned one lies tethered at your house; no milk, no nothing. When she dies, you can flay off her skin and sell it."

"Have you got some shame left? You don't even possess a dry-skinned one. You don't get a regular cup of tea, even."

"I don't know about tea. But if you're so proud of your strength, you can always test it out with me."

"Why, ask me if I have seen anyone as powerful as you? There are hundreds of them, really. Camel of the peels, that's what you're. Oh, I could easily carry you around my salwar strings. What are you talking, really!"

"Really! Then it's admirable."

Being embarrassed, this was about all Attra could manage to say. Who else but a bachelor like Attra would ever know the pleasures of having to suffer defeat at the hands of Bacchni in this manner! When Bacchni smiled at him mischievously, Attra felt like a mushroom in full blossom. It was difficult to say who was the winner, and who, the loser. Looking into Bacchni's eyes, Attra felt that she should keep talking to him in this manner, all day long, and that he should keep standing against the window, reclining. Bacchni had filled her basket up. While helping her lift the basket, Attra peered deep into her eyes, again, and he could feel a strange intoxication enter his pores as though he had had half a bottle. After helping her with the basket, he proceeded to the fields.

On nearing the fields, Attra turned back and saw Bacchni walk down as gracefully as a peacock, the basket full of dung-cakes resting upon her head. Her *chunni* was flowing in the air almost like the flag on top of a chariot. In the manner of an inebriated camel, Attra burst out into a song.

"*Oye*, bachelor, is everything all right? You really seem to be in a very different mood. Have you left something behind?" Jaila asked, as he came striding in.

"It's all right. What would happen to me? Not that anyone has sliced me with a *gandasa.*" Attra replied in a rather gruff manner as Jaila had thrown a spanner in his works.

"You look back as if someone is sitting, and gunning for you."

"Yes, my dear brother, you can afford to say all this. You have a wife as beautiful as an idol. If you don't talk, who will?"

Attra was also feeling piqued for another reason because Jaila had seen him stealing a look at Bacchni. Jaila had also caught him on the wrong foot. Smirking with his pursed lips, he said, "You also go and get yourself a wife. Why, is there a famine of women? These days, there is no end to the number of people who go to the camps just to ogle at women."

"If I get one from the camp, then people such as you would turn up their noses in disgust and say, 'you never know which caste he's got.' Then you'll go around circulating all kinds of stories about her. I'm better off without such a woman, really."

:"If you're so scared, get a *jatti*. Many, as tender as doe are still around. The parents looking for alliances often keep shouting from their roof-tops."

Attra had understood the deeper significance of his words.

"But what about people like you who are always waiting to play the spoil-sports? They simply go to the girl's parents, weave out a story as long as their beard and wink at them, asking them to keep everything under the wraps. Now even if someone were to agree for an alliance, he won't take long to change his mind."

"The spoil-sports don't want a cut from you, do they? Besides, you weren't born a cannibal that you couldn't marry early."

"That time also, it was no different. Bloody hell, they would quietly go and whisper into the ears of whosoever came, 'These bastards have no more than two and a half acres of land. What'll they feed your daughter, *pooras?*' And the fellow would beat a hasty retreat from the outskirts of the village itself."

"My dear brother, all this is the game of *karmas*. Not that you're going to be born to the rich parents now."

On hearing this bit about *karmas,* Attra felt really very angry as though he had been hit with a bamboo stick upon his head. As he had listened to this ridiculous thing about *karmas* all his life, he was quite tired of it. So much so that now he just could not tolerate the idea of anyone talking to him of destiny. Despite that, he had not taken the liberty to condemn this somewhat fatalistic attitude now. He had simply deflected the conversation by saying, "*Beliya,* what's there in the *karmas?*"

Attra responded in a dispirited manner, "All my life, I have been working so hard. Yet I don't have savings worth a penny. It looks as if I'm condemned not to see the face of a woman ever in my life. And bloody hell, the people who are good-for-nothing don't have one but two each, that too, as beautiful as fairies. I wonder where they hide the Book of *Karmas* when the turn of these people comes. You never know, they might have two entirely different Books. One would think I have crushed their fields of fodder that I'm being treated thus!"

"Isn't it much better? When you finally appear in the court of *Dharamraj,* you can always claim to be an ascetic!"

"That I will, won't I?" Attra chewed up his words as though

he was trying to hold something back, "If I ever have an encounter with Him, I'll definitely ask Him what His *gotra* is. Oh, I'm
sick of putting up with all His acts of waywardness!" They had
reached a small pathway running close to Jaila's fields. Jaila had
come to irrigate his lands. Before hitting the pathway, he fired his
parting shot, "And if you meet Him somewhere in the fields, you
must give Him a crushing blow on His jaw with this spade of
yours. After all, what does He think of Himself, that 'Godot?' He
should know how strong and youthful our Attra *jat* is!"

Though he had understood the meaning of what Jaila had
said, yet, having walked a little distance, he looked up at the metal
of the spade, resting upon his shoulder. As though he was trying
to gauge whether it would need more than a single blow to crush
the head of that stubborn 'God'....

Attra felt as though his entire body was burning with anger and resentment.

Clouds rose above the east and a cool draught of easterly
wind swept over him. Attra looked up at the sky, his eyes full of
hope. But that bit about the *karmas* that Jaila had mentioned
came back to haunt him. Heaving a deep sigh, he turned his gaze
towards the ground, 'Only if I had ten acres of land with a tubewell,
I would have raised the walls in goldbricks.' As he looked around
and saw a crop of cotton, rising as high as his waist, a longing rose
in his heart, too. He felt as though the cotton-flowers, as big as
lilac, were swaying in the breeze, breaking into a *giddha*. People
had irrigated their fields several times over but in his field, the crop
had barely risen as high as the palm of his hand. Since the big
landlords in the village used water from the irrigation channel for
irrigating their new fruit gardens, he had to wait for his turn rather
long.

Attra had only five acres of land out of which two acres
was barren. He often had to take five-seven acres on sharecropping basis and somehow grow enough to be able to provide for
everyone's daily needs. Attra was the one who had to look after
it all, single-handed. His elder brother was an opium-addict, so

he would have a little dose every day and sit in the village-assembly. On top of it, his *bharjai* was so short-tempered that she would not allow a housefly to settle upon her nose. All through the day, he would work like a black bull, and yet no one ever acknowledged his efforts.

'Why don't I give up this slavery and go off somewhere? I don't have kids wailing for me.' Occasionally, such thoughts would cross his mind, 'I work like a donkey all day long, and still no one appreciates.' The very next moment, he felt as though there was some magnetic pull about the village that was not allowing him to leave, and this pull was of his affection for Bacchni.

Bacchni was the wife of Attra's neighbour, Kartara. When she came to the village as a bride, Attra was about fifteen. She often used to tease him. Whenever he went to Kartara's house, she would always find one excuse or the other to talk to him. Being rather shy, Attra would invariably keep quiet. Bacchni had never addressed him by his name; she always called him *deora*. Slowly, Attra began to open up with her. Occasionally, he would even give a befitting retort to her witty comments. Then he developed some kind of liking for Bacchni. She had well-cut features, and was beautiful and tall, almost like a pine tree. Kartara was quite liberal in his attitude. He would often encourage Attra to play a game of dice with her, without suspecting either in the least. And Attra would also keep helping Kartara out, either by getting his plough repaired or bringing in a bundle of fodder for his cattle. As it is, Kartara was quite an easy-going person. But seeing them get so close to each other, Attra's *bharjai* would often gnash her teeth in helplessness.

Now Attra was on the wrong side of thirty. He certainly did not feel as youthful any more. Sometimes, he would feel rather depressed, but Bacchni would always pull him out by distracting him the way one would, a child. Attra was a very warm-hearted person but he was so naive that the boys would often call him 'Lola.' Even when he was a youth of twenty, no one had ever seen him leering at the girls. He would always remain self-ab-

sorbed. Seeing his youthfulness, many young brides would be
excited and tease him but he would never respond to their over-
tures ever. "Go along, you won't change ever, you egg-plant!"
They would say finally, giving up on him.

So far if there was anyone whom Attra recognised to be
his own, whom he had leaned on as a rock through these dreary,
drab thirty years of his life, it was Bacchni. All the other people in
the village appeared to be no more than strangers to him. Seeing
him walk down the street, they would often look at him as though
his biggest sin was being a bachelor. And the others he met would
either be sarcastic, just the way Jaila was, or gave him dirty looks.
Attra would feel as though a crowd of people, armed with sticks
and *gandasas,* had come rushing in to kill him; frightened and
breathless, he would go and hide his face in Bacchni's lap. Bacchni
would leap across at the crowd like a ravenous tigress. Attra felt
that all his life he should keep sleeping in her lap, but the commotion of the crowd, which sounded more like a volley of abuses,
would often create tremors in his heart. As he neared the fields,
Attra looked up. He felt as though the same crowd was trailing
him. Tremor ran through his entire body and then as though Bacchni
had wrapped him up in a blanket, he felt somewhat composed
now. Attra removed his clothes, hooked them up on the *beri* and
jumping across into the fields, started repairing the dyke.

The clouds that had come floating in from the east had
now drifted westwards. A little cloud passed over the sun, making it shine all the more brightly. As he dug into the grass with his
spade, it bounced back almost with the ease of a handball. When
he dug in, again, barely one-fourth of the blade could sink into it.
Attra was reminded of those days when it would hardly take him
much effort to jump across a four feet high wall, kicking the shoes
off it, in the process. He would not even tire when he had to
plough several acres of land at a stretch, but having borne the
burden of his brother's family, his limbs now appeared to be almost moth-eaten.

More than half the day had slipped away, though he had

not managed to repair even half the dyke so far. He was now beginning to get hunger pangs. Straightening up his back, he rested his hand upon the handle of his spade and started looking towards the fields of Karma. Santa's wife was carrying the *rotis* for him. And Attra felt as though someone were piercing his heart with a scythe. He could not quite make out whether the pangs were because of the hunger or something else. Leaving his spade there, he came and sat down under the shade of a *beri*. He looked in the direction of Santa's wife several times over. Perhaps it was the bright sun or whatever, he felt as though the stars were dancing before his eyes.

After a while, he got up with a start. Looking towards the small pathway leading up to his fields, he felt as though his exhaustion had suddenly lifted. Even the pangs in his innards were not so strong now. Shading his eyes with his hands, he cast another glance towards the pathway. And slowly the illusion turned into a palpable reality —Bacchni was walking in, *rotis* upon her head. It was as though his heart's desire had been fulfilled. As Bacchni drew near, he became increasingly oblivious of himself. So much so that he could not even get himself to think of any sweet-nothings to whisper unto her. It was as though his tongue had sealed off completely. Bacchni was only ten steps away from him, but he just stood there, bolt upright like the handle of his spade, staring at her.

"So you're standing, you, the inhabitant of hell!" It was as though by calling out to him first, Bacchni had resolved his dilemma, "O, you evil one, why do you work so hard? No one is going to offer you even a decent coffin. Then you earn for the sake of that 'goat' who treats you no better than a dog, when it comes to offering the crumbs! It seems, there is an old debt from some previous birth that you have to settle with her."

So overwhelmed was Attra with Bacchni's seemingly harsh though affectionate and love-soaked words that for a long time, he just could not think of anything to say. Going past him, Bacchni walked across to the shade of the *beri* and put the *rotis* upon the ground. But still quite lost, he was staring at her, almost in the manner of a wide-eyed bull.

"*Karmiya*, had you married, at least, it would have assured you food on time? It's already late in the afternoon and you're just burning your innards for nothing." Bacchni was pulling him up almost as if a mother were to restrain a child from wasting his time wandering about in the village. But Attra's heart was elsewhere, floating far beyond the range of Bacchni's words.

"*Bhabho,* I feel like swallowing you up." Attra spoke as though he had not heard a word of what Bacchni had said, "I swear by the cow, I feel such a strong pull towards you that if I had a horse, I would have kidnapped you just the way Mirza did."

"Come here, have a bite of a *roti* first. That is what you need right now. All this useless stuff can very well wait." Bacchni said as she offered him two butter-soaked *rotis* with pickle on top. He came and sat next to her, and sometimes he would stare at those butter-soaked *rotis* and sometimes, at her cheeks, as soft as butter.

"Why are you staring at my face? Do you see any flowers hanging there? Take these *rotis.* "

"There are no flowers hanging, I know. But I was just thinking that you look just the way you did when you had first come as a bride..."

"You'd better take *roti fist.* Talk later," cutting him short, Bacchni spoke with a harshness she never felt towards him. Despite herself, her suppressed smile, breaking out of her lips, had scattered, like the grains of hot-sand, upon her face, suffusing it.

Attra took the *rotis* from her, but he was not hungry any longer.

"Should I ask you one thing, *bhabho*?" Attra spoke almost like a petulant child, his face set close to hers.

"You ask that later. Right now, take any more *roti* if you want so that I could go. I have a long way to go. Since early morning, he has been weeding his cotton fields. He must be crying out with hunger already."

"These *rotis* are more than enough for me. But tell me one thing."

"All right, then, why don't you bark it off now?"

It was very difficult for Attra to hold back the thoughts that had been simmering inside him. So he spoke very softly, "What, if you were to marry me. ...?"

"You'd better not dream of such things." With these words she got up, her lips pouting as she spoke, "Throughout the day, you talk this silly stuff like some young man — your beard is turning grey now. You'd better start preparing for the cremation ground. Now we'll talk of marriage in our next birth. Besides, how can you claim someone else's wife." Bacchni turned her back and left.

It was as though she had left a storm brewing in his head. His eyes had begun to burn like embers. Though she was only a few steps away from him, he could not sight her anymore. For the first time in his life, Attra felt as though he was poised on the edge of an unbridgeable gap in his life, a gap he had crossed over in his life several times in the past but a gap he could not bridge anymore. Attra looked at the *rotis* that lay on his hands. They appeared to him to be more like the shredded dry-stalks of fodder. And he felt as though he had the body of a bull, 'I have wasted all my life. I worked like an animal, never did I act like a man! Like a bull, I have spent my life wandering in the fields. Is this life worth it? ...Bacchni is good but she is, after all, someone else's! Who is mine?....' And again, he felt as though the entire village was chasing him, bamboo sticks and *gandasas* in their hands. But now he could not find Bacchni's lap to hide himself in.

A sudden dread appeared in his eyes. He cast another glance at the *rotis* and then with all his might threw them against the stem of the *beri*. It was as if someone had shrieked within, "Why did you send me on this earth as a man. It would have been much better to be born a bull."

And for a long time, he had kept staring at the dust-laden

rotis. He wanted to hit his head against the stem of the *beri.* But
the soul of man was still alive within him, as it were. Holding his
arm and pulling him back, it was forcing him to graze the green
leaves of life for a few days more in the same fields where he had
been running around, fear-stricken, for more than thirty years now.
Yes, thirty years that seemed as long as aeons.

A Cattle Fair

Upon the mound itself, Bhuru Tangri of their village was busy massaging the sickle-shaped horns of his buffalo with oil, polishing them so hard as though he wanted to crush all the ticks that lay coiled around them. Every now and then, lifting his face up, he would look at the crowd of men and cattle ahead, wistfully as though he was still waiting for a customer to turn up.

Glancing in his direction, Santu told Pala, "Just look at him. Bai look at his legs!"

The moment his eyes fell upon him, Pala burst out laughing. Bhuru's legs were no different from that of a calf.

As soon as they came down from the mound, an altogether different world opened up before their eyes. On either side of a wide, open passage, an assortment of shops had been set up under the canopies. Spinning tops with springs, knives with white handles, rubber dolls, multi-coloured ropes, muzzle covers, jingling anklets, strings of bells – everything was there. Santu ran his hand through his pocket, had a feel of a four-anna coin and smacked his lips with his moist tongue. After a while, touching Pala's shoulder with his hand, he summoned up enough strength to say, "*Oye bai*, should we buy something to eat?"

"What do you want?"

"We could buy anything," said Santu, looking towards the tents rather hungrily.

"What do you mean, anything? Would you buy a camel or a horse? All you have is a change of an anna and a half."

"Why, I've four annas, to be precise!"

"All right. Let's go on ahead and have *jalebees*, then. But you'd better be careful. Don't lose it in the crowd."

Hearing him mention *jalebees*, Santu ran his tongue over his lips all over again and started peering in the direction of the huge tents. Sitting upon the wooden planks cut out of *keekar* and *beri* sat a few *jats*, eating out of big, bronze *thalees* resting upon old, won-out beams that had been raised with the help of a pile of bricks underneath. Santu was somewhat surprised, wondering whether it was the right time to have meals. Suddenly his eyes fell upon a man who looked rather overbearing but now sat swallowing big morsels. It was as if cutting a single morsel out of a *roti*, he was busy wiping the whole bowl clean of the *daal*. A thick pile, almost a foot high, of rotis as big as the griddle was lying right next to him.

"*Bai*, just look at him. The way that fellow is eating."

"Hardly eating, he is grazing, really!" said Pala, sneaking a glance at him as both exchanged smiles.

There was no shop selling *jalebees* in the vicinity. Of course, a balding *halwai*, as dark as a devil, was sitting under a worn-out, grimy tent, selling *makhane*, *kheelan*, *reorian*, and *batashe* spread in huge iron basins in front of him. Files and wasps buzzed over the *batashas* as though there was a honeycomb somewhere close by. Each time the *halwai* called out, hawking his wares, he appeared to be bleating like a young lamb. A squeaky voice coming out of his head, as big as a vessel, and his camel-like pouting lips, appeared somewhat strange.

"*Oye, bai*!" Santu called out to Pala very spontaneously, "Should we buy roasted sweet grams off that *rehriwala* for five paisa?"

"Forget it! Where did you find that fodder? It's fit for the cattle alone! Haven't you seen grams at home ever?" Pala looked at him, scowls creasing his forehead.

Lowering his gaze, Santu took his hand out of the pocket and grabbed it from outside.

Straight ahead stood a group of about fourteen-fifteen men, surrounding a man and shouting at him as though he had

stolen something of theirs. Clutching at the nose-ring of his emaci-
ated heifer in one hand, he was being dragged away be two men
who had grabbed hold of his other arm. One of them, with brown
moustache and blood-shot eyes, was trying to intimidate him over
and over again.

"*Oye*, are you a man or an animal? You'd better accept
the money quietly! Tommorow, no one is going to offer even half
a kilo of grams to this stupid fellow. Look at his face! He's de-
manding five hundred and fifty today! Thank your stars if you
manage to get rid of this 'diseased' liability!"

But the owner of the heifer was constantly rolling his head
around, saying "*uhoon-uhoon,*" time and again. Among the people
who stood surrounding him, many were staring at him, while the
mischief-makers were smiling all to themselves.

Towards the left, under the shade of the trees stood a
horde of cattle, stretching far into the distance-buffaloes, bulls,
cows and camels. Smell of fodder mingling with that of fresh dung
had spread all around. And this is what had begun to have almost
an inebriating effect upon Santu's senses.

Right ahead, under the *peepul* tree, was pitched the
canopy of Babaji. Shaking Pala's by his arm, Santu said, "*Oye
bai*! Let's go there and see the hippopotamus!"

"*Oye*, forget it! Are you the next of kin of a hippopotamus? It's nothing but a gathering of thugs there – don't you remember Inder *chacha* telling us how these people are always out
to dupe?"

Santu gave Pala a hurried, plaintive look and then started
gazing upon the canopy, again. All around the canopy sat several
young lads, crouched and huddled, almost like a pack of sheep
inside a vehicle.

Out of a loudspeaker, which was more like a broken-
down bucket, came the '*choon-chon*' of a song. Reclining against
a huge trunk sat babji sprawling, multicoloured medicine bottles
arranged neatly in front of him. His prominent, bulging paunch,
thick neck and a balding pate appeared somewhat strange. (Some

two years ago when, at the time of sowing of cotton, both the brothers had sneaked out of the fields to visit this very fair, *babaji* had not appeared half as healthy as he did now. Now, he looked more like Manna's brown bull). He couldn't get himself to glimpse either the dead hippopotamus or the stuffed crocodile-hidden as both these perhaps were behind the boys standing in the front.

"*Bai*! Should I go and have a peek at that?" mustering his courage, Santu asked Pala somewhat hesitantly.

But it was man selling strings of bells, coming in from the opposite direction who had caught Pala's attention. Santu too, found this man rather strange. With just a dirty piece of cloth wrapped around his waist, he had no footwear or a headgear. Hanging across his shoulder lay all kinds of muzzle-covers, jingling anklets and necklaces of green and red shells. His ribs and bones were sticking out, almost like the horn of a young calf. He would first hit the two jingling anklets, which he was holding in two of his hands, hard against the ground and then suddenly break into a call, "*Oye beliya*, take it along; take it along, O *beliya*." At the same time, jumping two steps on his toes and hollering "*hau*," in the manner of a heifer, he would move on ahead. Coming face to face with them, he burst into a discordant song, too, in his shrill, squeaky voice –

"Seeing the gait of a Punjabi girl

"The young lads start hollering!"

Despite himself, Santu started laughing. Twisting around, he asked Pala "What is he saying, *bai*|"

A smile playing upon his lips, Pala had kept staring at that man for a long time. But suddenly as if some fear had gripped him, shaking Santu's arm rather violently, he said, "O you bastard, hurry up and see whatever you want to. The day is about to sink."

Santu ran his gaze all around. However, he couldn't decide as to what he wanted to see and what he didn't ! Hurrying their pace, they took several rounds of the entire fair. At places, they just stood around and watched a few things in a somewhat more engaging manner, too. Santu must have turned around to

Pala, twice or thrice, for his advice on how to spend the four annas, but he didn't allow him to buy anything. Both of them were ravenously hungry. As they found themselves next to the fellow selling '*shardaai* with *ghunghroos*,' their thirst was whetted just as well.

"*Henh, oye, bai*, why is it known as '*sardaai* with *ghunghroos*'?" asked Santu.

"Can't you see for yourself? You drink it only after it's been crushed with a pestle adorned with *ghunghroos*."

Santu started laughing again. The fellow holding pestle would shake his leg to the beat of the *ghunghroos* almost in the manner of a heifer stung by a bee.

"Just look at him, *bai*, the way he's licking around – just the way our calf does." Santu burst into a loud guffaw.

With each movement of the sinking sun, Pala was becoming more and not les anxious. Dragging Santu by his arm, he said, "Let's go back to the village now. Otherwise, making scarecrows out of us, *bapu* will throw us upon the ant-infested mound. And once there, no one is going to bother for us."

Bapu's name was enough to send tremors through Santu's body as well. Once *bapu* got down to thrashing them up, he wouldn't stop until he had broken the stick into pieces. Santu had this feeling that their *bapu* had broken more sticks drubbing the two brothers than he had, beating his own bullocks.

The day was wearing itself out. Hurrying their pace, they returned home. But as they drew up next to a *rehri* selling roasted grams, Pala spoke up, without any prompting, "Want to munch popcorns?"

Feeling the four-annas inside his pocket, Santu nodded his head. But when the *rehriwala* was about to weigh the roasted grams, Pala suggested to him in a soft tone, "*Bai*, add a few sweet grams as well, say, worth about five paisa."

"Aha! Look at their faces. They want the sweet ones, too!" Though the *rehriwala* took his own potshot at them, he refused to concede to their request.

"This 'maternal uncle of mine' has hardly given us any-thing!" said Pala, as he stepped forward, spreading the lower part of his shirt to collect the roasted grams. Then darting an angry glance at the *rehriwala,* he divided the grams equally with Santu, each getting a share of no more than a fistful and a half. While still standing there, they filled their mouths by gobbling up a fistful each, and swallowing the half-digested grams like a person starved for long, they sped towards the village. They munched the rest of the popcorns while running off to the village. Out of this, too, Pala managed to pocket a few grams. Pestering him, Santu wangled those out of him as well. Then for quite a distance, they kept following the trail of the mud-dyke, munching the grams, rushing at a speed that would have certainly worn their *juttis* out. Biting into the grams in this manner as he went along, Pala was suddenly reminded of his calf feeding itself upon bits and pieces of the fod-der left behind in the manger. With a smile, he turned back but was unable to sight Santu anywhere around. When he shouted for him, Santu materialised from somewhere close to a young bull, gambolling like a deer.

"*Oye, bai, oye baï!* There is a notice pasted upon the wall of that vet hospital. The word 'bovine' is written upon it. Besides, it also has figure of a bull drawn upon it – Now what does this word 'bovine' mean?" asked Santu, finally catching up with Pala.

"First you get your breath back. As if you are the next of kin of 'the bovine creatures'! You hardly know the alphabet. And think as if you're the only 'studious one'!" With this shrewd jibe, Pala managed to cover up his own ignorance.

On reaching the mound, they slowed down, casting a lei-surely, backward glance momentarily. Far into the distance, the dark, shadowy, phantom-like figures of men and animals appeared to dissolve into each other. Peering into the darknes, Santu ws trying hard to figure out whether the men were dragging the cattle or it was the other way round. A few of the *jats* among them were lying down, their sheets spread underneath. Their calves and heifers stood around them, as if keeping a watch over them. As far as the eye could see, the sky was heavily dust-laden. The crimson of the setting sun mingling with the dust particles appeared to give the sky a somewhat menacing look.

"*Oye,* get along, now. Aren't you tired of watching it? Don't you know *bapu*? He'll simply beat the daylights out of us! Then your howling won't stop for a long time," said Pala chastising him for just idling around.

Dust-smeared legs of Santu began to tremble. And the naked soles of his feet appeared to give off heat. He ran and fell into step with Pala.

By the time they approached the village, the fair had begun to recede from their memory. Slowly, rising above the topmost boughs of the thick, heavy, phantom like trees, the ghostlike image of *bapu* appeared to be thinning out into the atmosphere.

"Oye, where did you get these four *annas* from? – Did you take it out of *bapu's* pocket?" queried Pala, as they went across the bridge over the tributary.

"Why would I do that? I had sold cotton."

"Then take it, your legs won't be spared today…"

It was as though that very moment Santu's body froze. But the very next moment, something like a whirlwind stirred within him. Getting restive like a heifer, he hollered, "Now, you just wait and see… I, too, will get him… well, into such a spin! After all, what does he think of us? Are we 'bovine creatures' in some fair or something?"

Grabbing hold of his empty pocket, Santu went hopping by Pala's side, frolicking around like a young lamb. Staring at him wonder struck, Pala was left way behind.

A Haunted House

Santi really used to like *bhaiji*. It was as though God had sculpted *bhaiji* during his leisure hours. Tall, well-trimmed body; sharp, well formed features; stubble on the chin and white complexion; even in the month of January his uncovered calf-muscles would keep blistering like *khichri*. Wearing a spotlessly clean white dress, sporting a pair of leather *jutti* and balancing a shining brass-stick when he passed through the street, the women would, on one pretext or the other, start staring out.

Santi could hear *bhaiji's* voice intoning *Satnaam* even from as far as four houses. Leaving her work aside, she would start washing her hands and feet, look at herself in the mirror, dust her clothes off and be ready by the time he came round. When *bhaiji* materialised outside the door and announced his arrival, holding a bowl of fresh milk and walking rather gingerly, often she would take her own sweet time to get to the door. Her eyes riveted on to his face, she would keep staring at his downcast eyes, which he never ever lifted, even for a while. Sometimes, she would dart a silly question across to him just to be able to look into his eyes, but he would respond, without lifting his gaze and then proceed to the next house to announce his arrival. Standing there, she would drag in deep sighs for awhile and then turn back, an empty bowl in her hand.

Sometimes, Santi would even be resentful of *bhaiji's* arrogance and think all to herself: 'the beauty which is the envy of the village boys, who're forever swaying over each others shoulders to catch its glimpse, is the one he never even lifts his eyes to see.' "What a sissy!" But the next day when she would hear *bhaiji's* voice intoning *Satnaam,* all the thoughts of the previous day simply vanished from her mind.

Within less than a month, Santi had became a regular visitor to the *Gurdwara*.

Even other girls had now started visiting the *Gurdwara* on a *masaya* or a *sangraandh*. A haunted place had started bustling with life, all over again. Santi, an infrequent visitor earlier, had now become as regular as the daily prayer.

Banta, Santi's husband, had been an opium addict 'right from his birth.' Sitting in the village assembly, all day long he would do nothing but take turns to push a pinch of snuff up his nostrils or break into loud, jarring snores. His father had left him something like ten acres of land, which he had given away on a sharecropping basis. And whatever fell to his share was more than enough to feed him and his family. Such an idler that he would leave home early, immediately after his morning cup of tea, and return only by the evening! After clearing up the dung and finishing the cooking, she would rush through her bath and be in the *Gurdwara* before sunrise. She would take Melu along. (After Melu, she hadn't had another child).

Once in the *Gurdwara*, Santi would be all ears, listening to *bhaiji's paath*. He would decipher the meaning of each and every word for her. On such occasions, she found him all the more handsome, making her want to hear the *paath* all day long. But seeing *bhaiji* steal furtive glances at his mother, again and again, Melu would glare at him and get restless, pressing his mother rather hard to return home early. When Santi refused to get up, he would start howling. Bhaiji would offer sugar bubbles to placate him but he always returned his gesture with an angry scowl. Finally, Santi would give in and return early, leaving her heart behind in the *Gurdwara*.

After about a month or so, people had started gossiping in the village. Each time she walked to the *Gurdwara*, holding Melu's finger, the women in her neighbourhood would start exchanging meaningful glances. Often, Santi would be in the know of what they were hinting at. Sometimes, it would even make her feel scared but the moment *bhaiji's* thought occurred to her, wrinkling her nose and curling up her lips, she would say, "I give a damn to all of them. Why should I take nonsense from them? Do they provide for us?"

Even the young lads of the village had now started looking rather suspiciously at both Santi and *bhaiji*. Sometimes, they would even start talking loudly to each other within his earshot distance, when he came on his daily rounds to collect food from different households, "O friend of mine! Strange are the tricks of the 'uncooked butter.' Pour it over a stick and it turns green. How can you blame the man when he slips?" But more than him, it was Santi they were really annoyed with, as she was the one who had shown her thumb to youth as tall as pine and decided to go ahead and have a liaison with this *bhaiji*, who was a novice, anyway.

So many times, even Banta had used it as an excuse to fight with her, but each time, Santi would come charging at him; she didn't like him in the least, now.

Sometimes, turning churlish, she would start muttering, "God knows where my parents got him from. He hardly looks like a man. I don't know what they saw in him; it would have been much better if they had just pushed me into a well!" But what could poor Banta do, he was quite fed up with her as it is. Every time he would go and sit in the village assembly, the people would direct all kinds of barbs at him, sharp as arrows. He was not a child either. As he understood everything, he invariably returned home feeling miserable and the emptiness of the house only compounded this feeling. That is the reason why now, for days on end, he would not be seen in the village at all.

And then, one day, the same thing happened that people had feared all along and were still gossiping about. The fire raging inside Santi leapt so high that even her maternal love for Melu failed to douse it. Leaving a settled house in ruins, she left with *bhaiji*. The people pounced upon Banta like a heifer, as if he was the one to be blamed for it all. '*Oye*, what kind of a man are you?

You should've shackled her down. Why couldn't you twist her plait around? Why couldn't you beat her black and blue until she lost her senses!' Showing off their own manhood, even the village elders wouldn't tire of taking jibes at Banta as and when they could. Often on hearing all this, Banta would quietly withdraw into his house.

For quite a few days, the young lads of the village kept gnashing their teeth over *bhaiji's* deed. 'Stitching her up, he's taken her away. Such a raging flame of fire that woman was! We fed him butter, but he's left all of us in disgrace!' Some of them were even annoyed with themselves over their own laxity.

Embarrassed, Banta left home on the pretext that he was going out in search of Santi. Holding Melu close to his chest, he kept roaming the streets of several towns, but she wasn't spotted anywhere. By the time he returned to the village, things had more or less settled down. It was as if the people didn't quite like the idea of inflicting more torment upon someone who was already tormented. Soon, this episode was consigned to memory and so was rarely ever revived now.

Now another *bhai,* who was much older and cleverer, had taken his position in the *Gurdwara.* He would even take time off to teach the village children. After mulling it over for a few days, Banta decided to send Melu over to *bhai* to study. As a result, he was almost tied down to the house. And Melu's presence alone was certainly not enough to cheer him up. So many times, he had even discussed the prospect of leaving Melu with one of his relatives, but who would have agreed to keep the son of such a wanton mother who had flown out of a well-laid nest.

And Melu kept growing, almost like an unprotected egg. Having lost all his interest in life, now Banta simply wanted to live for Melu's sake. All day long, he would be busy tending to his small needs. Over the years, Melu's tall height had become a natural staff for his age.

But as Melu was growing up, his temperament was undergoing a sea change. Sometimes, he would just beat up another boy of his age, without much reason.

Sometimes, he would burst into tears as soon as he returned home, and nothing would pacify him. Sometimes, he would leave home early and not return until late in the night, but Banta would never check him. So much of love he wanted to shower on him as would permanently heal the scars that the deprivation of maternal love had created in him. But the scars were becoming deeper and more conspicuous, every day.

Out in the fields, the boys were playing a stick-and-ball game. As he hit the ball with a stick, Tara hollered, "*Oye, bhaiji,* run and get it, now." But it wasn't Melu's ball but his stick, instead, that came flying through the air and hit Tara's ankles. And gritting his teeth, he screamed, "Call me *bhaiji* once again, O you son of mine!" All the boys were dumbfounded. Fearing trouble, a few of them ran off to their houses. Holding the stick, Melu was standing right at Tara's head while, lying in the sandpit, Tara was wriggling in pain like a snake.

In the evening, Tara's mother came to Banta with a complaint and he had to fold his hands to seek her forgiveness. But late in the night when Melu came home, Banta didn't ask him any questions. He was in a very foul temper and in such a state, he wouldn't have been able to make any distinction of an elder or a younger or observe any courtesies.

That night, Banta couldn't sleep at all. Even Melu kept tossing and turning in his bed.

The next morning when Melu was about to leave for school, Banta told him in a very gentle tone, "Son, by God's grace you're quite sensible now. You shouldn't really get into scrapes with people. What if, last night, that boy had been hit somewhere rather badly?"

"So what?" said Melu, anger showing through his voice, "Why do they mess up with me, then?" While collecting his bag, he first made a face and then left in a hurry.

Melu was now in the sixth class. He used to go to a high school in the adjoining village. The school was about two miles from their village. On the way, the boys would often tease him. If he decided to keep quiet, then throughout the way, he would walk in sullen silence, but if he happened to take an exception to someone's remark, he would bash him up rather badly. The boys had begun to understand him quite well now. When they saw him in an angry mood, they would steer clear of him. Even today, no one had really tried to needle him. On reaching the school, Melu didn't even go for the prayer meeting. He went to his room, straight. After the prayer, all the boys came into the class. The moment he walked in, the teacher busied himself with solving a mathematical problem, but Melu was still busy scratching the ink spots off his notebook's cover with nails. Suddenly, the lead in the pencil of Natha, who was sitting right next to Melu, broke. Turning to Melu, he blurted out impatiently, "*Bhaiji,* your pen...."

Half the sentence was still stuck in his throat when Melu's punch landed on his sides. Natha let out a scream and instantly, everyone turned around, confused.

"What's wrong with you Nathiya?" asked the teacher, staring at Natha and Melu, who was sitting, his eyes downcast.

"*Ji*... he's given... me... a punch," spoke Natha through his sobs.

The teacher's eyes turned blood-shot. Ever since the session got underway some two months ago, Melu had, without much reason, beaten up around five to six boys in the mathematics class itself. Being of a very different temperament, this teacher had not made any effort to punish Melu for his acts of indiscretion. He wasn't really in a habit of chastising his students. But today, he was shaking with rage.

"Melu, did you hit him?" he queried, but Melu kept sitting still.

"Why don't you stand up?" he asked again, his voice choking with anger; but Melu kept sitting as usual.

"I said, you stand up. Did you hear me or not?" The teacher nearly screamed.

"I won't," replied Melu, looking straight into the teacher's eyes that were burning like charcoal. Now whether it was anger or fear that paralysed him temporarily was difficult to say, but for awhile, at least, he couldn't get himself to think of anything to say.

"All right, pick up your bag and quietly walk out of the room." His voice was harsh still, though his limbs had become rather lifeless.

"I won't go." It appeared as though Melu's eyes would soon start dripping blood. For some time, the teacher kept standing there, but finally returned to the black-board. So dumbfounded were the boys that they just kept looking at the teacher and Melu, by turns. And the teacher started explaining the same problem as though nothing had happened.

Melu's body had begun to burn like a piece of hot iron. His eyes were flashing embers. It became almost impossible for him to keep sitting there, even a while longer. But throughout the period, he sat there with his eyes downcast. That moment, he wished that the earth would split open and swallow him within its bowels.

When the bell rang, stomping his feet, he walked out of the classroom and headed straight for the village. All along the way, he didn't lift his head even once.

As soon as he reached home, he fell down flat on the *manji*. Even the neighbours heard his cries and sobs but as they knew him to be generally a miserable creature, no one paid much attention to him. (As the matter pertaining to the land was to be settled, Banta had gone to the adjoining village to meet the *Patwari*). Until the evening, Melu was either crying or thinking all kinds of strange thoughts.

In the evening, he got up and cooked a meal for himself. Leaving four *rotis* for Banta in the tray, he decided to carry the rest with him. Taking out thirteen *annas* from under the earthen pitcher, he tied them into a knot of his turban and stalked out. It was already dark, a time to light the *diyas*.

He went and stood outside the *Gurdwara* in such a way as though someone had tied his feet down. Peering above the low wall, he saw that *bhaiji,* carrying the incense in an earthen plate, was offering it to *Nishaan Sahib.* Melu kept standing there for a while. It was as if someone was sloughing him off from within. Then picking up a sod, he threw it across the wall, aiming the *bhai.* The incense plate fell off *bhai's* hand and he sat down upon the platform itself. With his hand resting upon his forehead, he started spouting vulgar abuses.

And running wildly, Melu hit the road leading to town.

Within a few minutes, this incident had spread across the entire village like wild fire. On returning home late in the night, when Banta learnt about it, cold shivers ran down his spine. By reminding him of the past incidents, the people had started rubbing salt into his wounds.

And that night Banta entered his house, never to leave it again. After about a fortnight, people had removed his corpse from inside. Even those friends and relatives had come to join in the funeral procession who hadn't otherwise bothered to enquire after him even once during the fortnight. His distant *bhabhis,* as far removed as those of the third generation, too, beat up their breasts so severely as to turn them crimson.

The sons of his *chachas* and *tayyas* arranged a great funeral for him. Banta didn't have a single real brother of his own. A day after the *Dussehra,* his relatives drew up plans to divide his land amongst each other, and had his other stuff also carted to their houses. For several months, Banta's funereal house continued to be the subject of discussion among the people, but slowly it all subsided and died out. Thereafter, it was very rarely that anyone ever mentioned Banta. It was as though, while going past his abandoned house, needles would start stabbing people's eyes. Now this house had begun to appear more like a cremation ground, inhabited by the ghosts, and so the people trembled each time they went past it.

Late in the evening, people saw a crazy fellow running around in the streets of the village. Barely out of his teens, he was quite good looking though his ragged clothes and dishevelled hair did give him a rather frightful appearance. Scared, the women hustled their children inside. Seeing his appearance, a few young-sters ran and got themselves sticks before chasing him around, which they did with such vigour as though a mad dog had strayed into the village.

He would go around peeping inside the people's houses and then start screaming at the top of his bent. After letting out a scream, he would run to the next door and stand there, transfixed. The moment he came close to the courtyard of Santu, the lame one, he suddenly took to his heels and then stopped only once he had let himself into the empty cottage of Banta, the addict. Equipped with sticks and *gandasas,* the people kept pouring into the street outside.

After a while when that crazy fellow came out, shouting and screaming, he had a moth-eaten, pillar of a tub in his hand. Scared stiff, people beat a hasty retreat. As soon as he was out of the door, he sped away towards the *Gurdwara.* And the people almost attacked him.

But much before people could intervene, the crazy fellow had torn both the legs of *bhai* and smashed them as well.

All the people fell into a single swoop upon him. A few of the youngsters punched and kicked him as well, but the elders immediately intervened to stop them from doing so. Half of the people went rushing to *bhaiji's* aid while the others tied up the arms of the crazy fellow. After a while, when they saw his face in the light of a *diya,* almost everyone let out a deep sigh — he was Banta's Melu.

That night, no one slept in the village. Like the sound of thunder in the month of *Jeth,* Melu's screams had kept piercing the hearts of the people, all through the night. The women of the village kept talking about Banta's abandoned house, which was now believed to be the abode of ghosts and where the screams of a ghost continued to be heard until the crack of dawn.

A *Kareer* Branch

Last night, once again, Balwanto's father-in-law and brother-in-law, Maghi, had got drunk and shouted abuses at her. Her grown up daughter was standing by her side. (But her presence had not shamed the father-son duo, in the least). Both her sons, who were much younger, had quietly slid into the bed and lain there, crouching under the quilt, almost like pheasants, fear looming large in their eyes. And lying close by, though Gyala had quietly listened to it all, like a demure woman, something had really whirled inside him, making him restless. Last night, she had, again, been reminded of the promise she had made to Gyala but this time she had not been able to get herself to brush it aside, saying, "We'll think about that another time." For the past several months, she had found it increasingly difficult to say so as her anger had invariably threatened to spill over.

This was certainly not the first time that her father-in-law and brother-in-law had flung abuses at her. For over twelve-thirteen years now, each time they got sozzled up, all they did was spout abuses. So far not even once had she spoken disrespectfully to anyone. Such louts, they probably thought that the only way to enjoy their drink was to start shouting the choicest of abuses! (If she had her way, she wouldn't even like to abuse an animal, fearing that this act of hers might be misunderstood). Earlier she used to lump it all but now in the presence of her grown up daughter, she found it extremely difficult to tolerate the idea of such good-for-nothing louts heaping abuses upon her.

That night, Balwanto didn't get even a wink of sleep. It

was as if someone had first off-loaded a handful of *kareer* thorns inside her and then with a sudden kick scattered them all. She couldn't even get herself to turn her side. The thorns kept tearing apart each and every limb of hers. Well past the mid-night, her eyes had remained moist, almost like the stars in monsoons. But slowly, after mid-night, turning dry, her eyeballs had begun to burn and sear. So strong was the radiation of the heat that her eyes had closed without much effort on her part. But when her eyes opened again, she suddenly got up with a start.

Day light had spread all around. Gyala was busy feeding the cattle. Her elder daughter was preparing to boil tea. As she looked around with her tired, sleep-laden eyes, everything appeared strange to her. She felt as though the burden of sleep would shut her eyes on its own. Rubbing her eyes with her palms, when she suddenly held her hands up, she felt as though mulberry glue was sticking to them. After a while, dusting her hands off, she started rubbing the eyes again. (For the past two years, each time she rubbed her eyes, it felt as though she was snuffing her beauty out, almost like the last splinter in the ear of the corn. Every time it felt as though the grains of her beauty were slowly flaking off, leaving the husk behind, empty and hollow husk, which, too, had now been scattered away, what with the crows and sparrows muzzling their beaks against the pile.)

After her marriage when Balwanto had just come into the house, the onlookers had been left speechless by her beauty. Even Sodhan, the barber's wife, who had the reputation of being the most unsparing of all the critics in the village, had not been able to point out a single flaw in her. She hadn't been able to find an apt metaphor to describe her beauty. All such expressions as 'like a fairy,' 'like an idol' or 'queen of flowers' she had found completely bare of meaning. And finally she had said, "Poor jats have somehow stumbled upon a real ruby." She actually thought that her eyes were as flaming red as a ruby. But today, when fourteen years had slipped away, her eyes had become empty as seashells! Now the rays radiating from this ruby had lost their sheen to such an extent that nothing was reflected in them any longer, neither the image of anything deeper inside nor that of anything outside. It was as though fourteen years of dust had settled on either side, dimming their light.

After feeding the bullocks, Gyala came and sat down next to the *chulha*. Jeeta, their elder daughter, brought in a mug of tea and placed it in front of him. The moment Gyala put the mug to his lips, Jeeta darted such a look at him that he couldn't dare to return the stare. Then he cast his eyes down. But Jeeta had kept staring, sometimes at his deep-set eyes and sometimes, at his straggly beard.

Whatever may have been behind the look that the father and the daughter exchanged, the moment it caught Balwanto's eye, such a heavy sigh escaped her lips that she had to stuff her mouth with a corner of her *chunni*. When the same thorns pricked Balwanto's insides, it was as though each and every pore of hers was groaning in pain. Sitting stock-still, she fell down flat upon the *manji*. (As Gyala was sitting with his back towards her, he hadn't noticed anything).

After finishing his tea, Gyala left for the fields with a view to weed out the cotton crop. Jeeta attended to everything in the house, from cleaning up the dung to cooking the meals and carried the *roti* to the fields as well. Balwanto kept lying on the *manji*, impassively. She didn't have her meals either. And the younger ones quietly left for school on their own. As the emptiness in the house was beginning to gnaw at her, Balwanto got up so that she could throw herself into some kind of work. But the moment she got off the *manji*, the first thing that she saw was the turban of her father-in-law tipping above the common wall. Once again, the thorns that lay scattered inside her started tearing her limbs apart. Balwanto lay down upon the *manji*, again, totally oblivious of the promise she had made to Gyala.

Ever since she had stepped into this house as a bride, her mother-in-law had been constantly nagging her. And the barbs that she threw at her most frequently had to do with dowry. 'Are we gypsies that they should hurl such silver anklets in our faces...?' What are we going to do with her beauty, lick it on our palms?' Though for a long time, she hadn't uttered such malicious words to Balwanto's face, the way her mother-in-law often criticised her to the ladies in the neighbourhood was something that she would eventually get to hear from them. On her part, Balwanto had tried her best not to ever give her a cause for complaint. She would do all the household chores, tirelessly. She would cook for ten members of the family, tend to some eight or ten cattle-heads, not allow anyone in the family to wear dirty clothes ever and keep the house as clean as a churning vessel. And yet, there seemed to be no respite against her mother-in-law's barbs, which were becoming more caustic by the day. That was more than enough to break her heart. Slowly when, on one pretext or the other, she started venting ıer spleen on Balwanto, her patience almost caved in.

One night, she decided to tell Gyala everything. But Gyala was more of an 'effeminate' man. He told her very gently, "Ever since I was born, I haven't been insolent to my parents even once. If you were to answer them back now, my life's efforts shall go waste. Do whatever you will, but never should you answer back my parents – never in your life."

And Gyala had extracted a promise from her that she would never act in an insolent manner in presence of his parents. About this promise, Balwanto felt as if in a field awash with water, someone had suddenly thrust a *kareer* branch in front of a small rivulet to stem its flow... That is how her innards, too, like a parched field, had first yearned for water and then started cracking up.

For full three years, she had endured the barbs and the malicious comments of her mother-in-law, rather demurely. She even put up with the comments and abuses of her drunkard father-in-law and her good-for-nothing brother-in-law, but not even once did she break her promise. (Right from day one, she had felt so much of pity and compassion for Gyala that now she felt protective towards him almost like a mother. And this compassion had grown into such a strong attachment now that she could sacrifice almost anything for Gyala's sake)

Then her brother-in-law got married. His wife brought in a fat dowry, so much so that the entire house was flooded with things. That made Balwanto lose whatever little respect she had earned through her own efforts. She often told Gyala that they should go in for a division of the family assets and set up their own house. However, he continued to ignore her warnings until such times as they were virtually driven out, with all kinds of wild accusations heaped upon them and the label of a 'henpecked husband' sticking to him.

Even at the time of division, Gyala didn't do anything that showed signs of real masculinity in him. His father didn't even give him his regular share of the land; what ultimately fell to his share was a piece of useless land, infertile and full of wild overgrowth. Out of the house, too, he was given only one fifth of the total share. The bullocks he got were old, and the implements almost useless. They even decided to keep half of the utensils and clothes that Balwanto had got from her parents' house. Gyala had refused to speak up for his rights and Balwanto had remained true to her word, both exercising the utmost restraint.

Now for the past eleven years, they had been exercising nothing but the restraint. And it was the twelfth year when, as they say, the petition of the dung heap is also heard. But theirs had still not been heard. Half crumbled, their house lay in a bad state of disrepair, as they hadn't been able to use, why, not even the unbaked bricks for repairs. Even the shed where the cattle were exposed to the direct sun in the scorching heat of May and June was no better. So old was the straw roof above the manger that with the sun beating down it would start sizzling in the heat rather than offer protection to the cattle. The small store at the back was only a shade worse. Almost every year, during the monsoons, it would be flooded with rainwater. (Balwanto would try her best to keep the house in order; but her efforts alone couldn't have possibly transformed almost half a century old walls and woodwork in the house). After the split, they hadn't bought a heavy buffalo or an

energetic bull. Gyala hadn't been able to get even the rubber on
the wheels of the cart replaced. Every time he simply got a sheet
of rubber put on the old wheels, repairing them in much same way
in which one would repair a pair of old *jutti,* and keep dragging
the cart around. (So much so that now people had, in half jest,
started referring to it as Gyala's *nagauri* cart).

For eleven years, she had put up with all sorts of wild and
not so-wild accusations and reproaches of her mother-in-law, her
father-in-law and other kinsmen. But not even once had she
allowed that *kareer* branch to break, one that Gyala had plugged
in by way of a promise. As a lot of things, such as bits and pieces
of straw had got stuck to it, thickening it over the years, the flow
of water had been completely blocked out. And this rather long
drawn out drought had split her insides open, almost like a
muskmelon.... Dashing against it hard, sometimes, the water
would almost threaten to break the *kareer* branch....

As if what the others said was not enough, her sister-in-
law, who behaved more like a *sauten,* would forever be ready to
tongue-lash her. God alone knows what kind of a family she had
come from that, once convinced of how vulnerable Balwanto's
position really was, she had started baring her fangs more and
more. Each time, any of Balwanto's children cried out for
something, it pleased her no end. And whenever Gyala and
Balwanto had an altercation or a verbal duel, it invariably gave
her peace and satisfaction. Her ears glued to the walls, she would
try and overhear everything and then circulate the inner story all
around, making mountain out of a molehill.

Initially, Balwanto hadn't been able to figure out why her
sister-in-law behaved towards her in a manner she did. One day,
her sister-in-law's father made a sudden appearance and left a
healthy calf tethered to the post. When Bachinti's daughter-in-
law, her neighbour, came to congratulate her, she didn't give her a
straight reply. Rather, peering over the wall with a squinted eye,
she deliberately spoke in a voice loud enough to be heard by
Balwanto, "By God's grace, there's no dearth of anything. We

have seven such calves as strong as she-elephants. So *bapu* said, 'Child, take whichever you like.' ... After all, we won't have to go begging for *lassi* from door to door, as some people have to!"

And that's when things had fallen in place for Balwanto. Her parents' riches had made her sister-in-law really swollen-headed. And that's what gave to her a decisive edge in her in-laws' family as well. No wonder, she had always treated Balwanto as someone only a shade better than an insect or an ant.

For the first time, it occurred to Balwanto, 'Had I been the daughter of well-to-do parents, I, too, would have got myself a buffalo from there and tied her in my courtyard. At least, I would have been spared this humiliation.' But she knew her parents were not even in a position to give her clothes and other odd gifts. (Such were the moments when she really condemned herself for being so poor).

...Slowly the water table started rising. It had now begun to put a good deal of pressure upon the *kareer* twig, but the wild overgrowth that lay clinging to it had not allowed it to break. So much so that the inner landscape of Balwanto had turned completely drought-ridden, leaving the roots of the grass to singe in the sweltering heat.

Stock-still, Balwanto kept lying on the *manji* all day long. Late in the evening when Gyala returned home, seeing her in bed, his heart nearly leapt into his mouth. (It was as if in course of a single day, Balwanto's beauty had lost all its lustre. Her eyes had sunk and the dark circles beneath them had thickened so much as though smudged with charcoal. Her face, hands and feet had turned the colour of turmeric, pale and vapid yellow).

Dispirited, Gyala sat down upon the manger. His back and head had begun to ache a lot. As his head was swimming, he bent down to rest his head upon the handle of a hoe. Sliding into a dream-like state, he started musing over those very features of Balwanto which had an irradiating glow about them, only fourteen years ago...! (Thinking her to be as delicate and fragile as a doll, and almost as white as the soft, butter paper, he wouldn't ever hold her hand for the fear that it might spoil her complexion… or who knows it might even sprain her hand….)

The moment Gyala lifted his head to look up, his eyes fell upon Maghi wandering about, hair in a total disarray. In a fit of drunkenness, he was staggering about the place. The moment he saw Gyala sitting upon the manger in this sad posture, tiptoeing, he first looked around and then in a sarcastic tone, asked rather loudly, "So tell me, O soul mate of mine! What kind of thoughts are you lost in?" His voice was gruff, devoid of any emotion.

Gyala had never had any discussion with him. Eleven years had gone by since they had been separated. It was difficult to say how many times, since then, this incorrigibly drunkard, younger brother of his had reproached him, had had digs at his expense, directed all kinds of barbs at him or abused Balwanto rather brazenly; but not even a whimper of protest had escaped Gyala's lips ever. Drinking it all in, he would invariably withdraw inside. Even today, he did very much the same. When Balwanto, who was lying in the shadow of the store, saw him enter in this manner, her innards, ravaged by a drought of a decade and a quarter and already split like a muskmelon, suddenly cracked open with an intense, scorching heat…. It was as if sun had rained all its burning heat over it.

Sitting upon the *manji*, Balwanto couldn't spot anyone except her tipsy father-in-law. (Laughing rather crudely, Maghi had tiptoed to the other side). With her deathly eyes, she looked at him in such a manner as though she was looking at the messengers of *Dharamraj* who had come to fetch her. (For a very long time, it didn't even occur to her that she shouldn't sit bareheaded in the presence of her father-in-law. While she was trying to heave herself up on the *manji*, her *chunni* had slipped off her head but she hadn't made the least effort to put it back in place).

…And finally the promise, which was stuck inside her almost like a *kareer* twig, had split into splinters. Out came the water, gushing from a decade long drought-ridden land, washing away the *kareer* twig and much more that lay sticking to it. It was as if the floodgates had been thrown open and overrun with water, the cracked surface of the land inside, though as solid as the boulders, had suddenly shrivelled up into cracks, all over again....

"You bloody..." Seeing her sitting bareheaded, her father-in-law shouted a filthy abuse at her, "You've reduced me to just another pimp! ...I'll slice you up into pieces and dump you somewhere. No one would even get the wind of it. Don't you give yourself airs unnecessarily!"

But this time, hearing her father-in-law's voice, Balwanto didn't flinch in fear as it always used to happen in the past. She neither lifted her *chunni* to cover her head nor did she lower her gaze. Rather brazenly, she just kept staring at her father-in-law.

"What's the matter?" asked Maghi, sidling up to him as he heard his father spout abuses.

"Now look at this bloody prostitute. How brazen she is? As if all the misdeeds she did until now were not enough, she has done this as well. Just look at this shameless one! The way she's sitting. Almost like a prostitute...Get me a *gandasa* for a minute. Let me put an end to this business once for all."

"Why do you want to sully your grey beard? Let me do this good deed and earn the reward. Besides, it'll save my brother from this daily torture...I'm going to relieve him off this 'burden' around his neck...!" hollered Maghi, tying his loose hair into a top-knot.

Climbing on to the manger and jumping across the wall, he came into her courtyard. Shouting imprecations, Balwanto's father-in-law, too, came in, entering through the door in the street. On hearing the commotion, Gyala stepped in from inside his house and seeing the demonic faces of his father and brother, he immediately cringed.

...But now the *kareer* branch lay broken.

Much before they could lay their hands upon her, hollering, she sprang to her feet. All of a sudden, her sunken eyes had turned blood-shot. Her head still uncovered, she picked up the pestle lying in a corner and screamed at the top of her voice –

"Come on, you bloody brothers-in-law of my father! I'll see now who dares to come anywhere near me… Try and touch me if you want, then I'll dig into your intestines and scoop them out…!"

So loud was her scream that even Gyala failed to recognise her voice. Wincing in fear, the younger children had retreated against the wall, bursting into tears. Gyala's father and Maghi, too, were somewhat overawed. They simply couldn't believe that she was the woman who, for twelve long years, had endured all their insults, their harsh words and abuses like an impenetrable wall. And now the same woman had appeared in the incarnation of *Kalka mai*, holding a pestle and swearing revenge against her tormentors. This had appeared rather strange even to their drunken eyes. But the very next moment, those very drunken eyes had turned ferocious without so much as a flicker of a thought. Almost like hungry lions, both the father and the son had pounced upon that "prostitute of a woman."

"Balwanto!" Gyala shouted as he ran towards her.

But Balwanto! …Now which Balwanto was he talking to? …Balwanto was nowhere around …The *kareer* branch had already been ripped apart…!

Gyala had not even managed to reach anywhere near her, when rushing headlong towards Maghi, she hit his right shoulder so hard with the pestle that his arm, like a chopped-off branch, had begun to dangle loosely by his side. And the moment the father-in-law stepped forward, leaving Maghi aside, she turned around and attacked him. As a light stroke of the pestle hit him as well, he backed away, mouthing filthy abuses, and came into the backyard looking for a stick or a staff with which he could defend himself. Though by this time Gyala had managed to rush on ahead and inch closer to Balwanto, having jumped back, she was now standing with her back against the wall. Standing in that position, she hollered out, once again,

"Now let anyone of you, my bloody kinsmen, come

anywhere near me…! For fourteen long years, you burnt my insides
out – just because I was a woman? …Try and come near me now
and you'll have me sucking your blood …Besides, go and call
that 'daughter' of yours whose 'king of a father' used to bring a
'she-elephant' for you each time he came…You wretched people!
You who feed yourself on offal! If you really were born to men,
then accept the challenge of this daughter of a 'destitute'…! For
fourteen years, I did nothing but listen to what you had to say…And
you left nothing to chance when it came to tormenting my soul…!
Come near me now, why don't you? Come and see what a hand
woman deals you now…I'm going to suck each and every drop
of your blood." All of a sudden, her face became so ruddy and
flushed as though she had just about finished drinking a bowl full
of blood. No one could muster courage to come anywhere near
her.

On hearing the commotion, the people from the immediate
neighbourhood came rushing in. The moment their eyes fell upon
Balwanto, standing with a pestle in one hand, shouting abuses at
the top of her bent, most of them just hung their heads in shame.
Some of them, especially those who were resentful of Gyala's
father and Maghi, kept smiling all to themselves. Inder, the
lambardaar, was going red in the face with embarrassment and
anger, as he had not set eyes upon such a shameless woman ever
in sixty years of his life. When the sight of a woman mouthing such
abuses became virtually intolerable for him, pulling the weight of
his age and authority, he stepped forward, hollering,

"Will you stop it or not? …You behave like a prostitute's
daughter…What has bitten you?"

When he stepped forward a little, another loud scream
escaped Balwanto's lips:

"*Baba*, you'd better watch out! Don't you lose your
'turban'! Go and worry about your *lambardaari*… O you
protector of justice! By the way, where were you when these
people were arranging my 'funeral'? …Were you residing in this
village or some other, then?"

The *lambardaar* nearly bit his tongue in surprise.

And then suddenly the tables turned. Inder, the *lambardaar*, almost pounced upon a shocked Gyala, standing in a corner. "You bloody fool! What kind of a man are you? How indulgent are you of this she-monkey! You want the entire village to lose its honour for the sake of such sheep? O you bloody dog! Aren't you ashamed of yourself?"

And within minutes, forgetting Balwanto, everyone had turned against Gyala. People swooped down upon him, almost like vultures hunting a rat.

"O you bloody call yourself son of a man!"

"If he had any sense, he wouldn't have really spoilt his 'woman' so much?"

"He's bloody useless, worse than a woman, really."

"If my woman had done such a thing, I would have buried that bitch alive!"

"How dare a woman open her mouth? If she does it, just catch her by the plait and give her four tight whacks on the face. Enough to straighten her out like a spindle...."

When Gyala overheard such harsh and hurtful words, it appeared to him as though he was seeing a dream. It was the mention of the word 'woman' that had made him feel as though hundreds of men were holding his arms and pulling him in two opposite directions in a tug-of-war. (Balwanto was the same woman who had given up practically everything for his sake, so much so that she had even wasted herself away to please him. Sometimes, he felt as though she was the real source of life for him – almost in the same manner in which the king in the folk tales is said to have his life source in a parrot hanging upon a tree ... And what all didn't these people say about 'woman'?) Gyala felt as though he was going to lose his consciousness. He was on the verge of losing his sanity as well.

Ultimately, realising that it just might take a turn for the worse, the village elders forcibly took Gyala's father and Maghi away from the scene. Almost everyone abused the 'effeminate'

Gyala of Balwanto to their heart's content and went their way.
Though the commotion of the courtyard had spread all through
the village, Balwanto still stood there, her back against the wall.

     Mortified with shame, Gyala had walked back into the
house. (He hadn't even realised when and how he suddenly broke
into a smile. Seeing this rather strange and unfamiliar smile, the
children, who were already petrified, sank into a complete silence).

     ...Then suddenly he heard a loud thud outside, as if a
withered branch of a tree, struck by the whirlwind, had fallen. He
ran out. Balwanto was lying on the ground, her face down.
Carrying her into his arms, he brought her back into the house.

     And on the seventh day, thereafter, people heard that
Balwanto had died.

Price of a Bride

It had hardly been four or five days since Maghar brought his wife home when Santi saw Pakhar at Maghar's house, drinking and laughing heartily. Santi felt as though all the seven pieces of her garments had been set afire. When Pakhar returned home dead-drunk at mid-night, Santi charged at him like a lioness.

"And in future if I ever see you crossing the threshold of these people, I'll flay everyone's skin alive, and that, of course, includes you also." Livid, Santi had growled at him.

Without saying a word, Pakhar had just looked at her with his inebriated eyes. Then he picked up the pitchfork lying beside the bowl and hurled it across at Santi. As he was unsteady, it missed Santi by a few inches. When he went staggering in to pick it up again, Santi mustered a little courage and gave him such a hard push that he lost his balance and fell upon the *manji* like a rock. Lying there helplessly, he kept bad-mouthing and abusing Santi for a long time. Disturbed by so much of commotion, the children had woken up, startled, and started crying and wailing louder than ever.

This was the first unfortunate night in their house. They had been married for fourteen years. The same Pakhar who never ever used to address her informally with an 'oye' now had the least hesitation in showering the choicest of abuses on her. Every now and then, he would get drunk and start beating her up. And Santi, who was not in the habit of speaking loudly even to the strangers, would now go around snarling at almost everyone she ran into. Even after having been beaten up and abused by Pakhar, she would hardly ever shut her mouth. She would start saying whatever came to her mind and that is how things had gone from bad to worse. And a happy home had turned into a living hell.

Maghar was Pakhar's elder brother. As he was somewhat naive and simpleton right from the beginning, and as there was also wretched poverty in the house, he had not been able to marry. Ever since Pakhar had got married, Maghar had been eating at his house. Then some years ago when, on being incited by his parasite-friends, he had sought separation from Pakhar, it hadn't taken him long to sell off most of his land and blow away the money. Whatever three-four acres were left, he sold those too, and bought himself sheep. Slowly, when all his parasite friends had deserted him, he came back, cringing for refuge at his brother's house. As he was a real brother, so Pakhar had to take him in. Though Santi was not in favour, Pakhar had somehow made her agree to it.

After sometime, he was back again with his parasite-friends. This time round, they divided the house and had a wall raised in the middle. Then within a few days, they had made this 'moon' appear all of sudden. After selling off his sheep, they had bought him a bride from somewhere. Santi somehow got to know that Pakhar, too, had a hand in it. She had tried to engage him in a conversation and draw him out, but he just wouldn't breathe a word about it.

Hardly had Maghar's wife stepped in, when Santi's house became a living hell. The very next day, Santi found a sudden change in Pakhar's temperament. And when she saw him drinking at Maghar's house, her worst suspicions were confirmed.

Since that day, Santi had begun to look upon Maghar's wife as a bundle of poison.

Sometimes she felt so enraged that she just wanted to hack this 'ebony-faced witch' into a thousand pieces. Out of sheer resentment, she would sometimes stand in the backyard and start fomenting her torrent of abuses. It was difficult to say what kind of a strange woman she was, for not even once had she stooped down to give Santi as good as she got. Whenever Santi would start her volley of abuses, she would immediately go inside. Santi hadn't even seen her face properly. Sometimes, Santi felt as though she were fighting against the wall. When her anger subsided, she would feel extremely embarrassed. But the moment she set her eyes upon Pakhar, the fire of anger, inside her would be stoked all over again.

Maghar's wife had not even completed one month in the house when Pakhar had already beaten up Santi several times over. Last night, he had battered her so badly that even in the day time now she could see the stars dancing before her eyes. She hadn't been able to get up in the morning to give fodder to the cattle, something she used to do every day. Early in the morning when Pakhar had left for the fields, his bullocks still hungry, she had kept wailing in the bed for a long time.

Now the sun was about to set, Pakhar had not yet returned from the fields. The children had gone out to play. Lying upon the *manji,* when Santi looked across the dividing wall, she glimpsed the head of Maghar's wife above it. It was as though something like molten iron began to simmer inside her and the flames leapt out of her body.

The very next moment, Santi got up from the *manji* like a maelstrom and came into the backyard. Picking up the chopper lying in the backyard, she clambered up on the manger and jumped across the common wall, into Maghar's courtyard. "O rival of mine! You'd better get ready now. Today, I'm going to scoop your heart out and eat it." She screamed, savagery showing through her voice, as she menacingly brandished the chopper, rushing in towards Maghar's wife. Seeing the dreadful expression in Santi's eyes, Maghar's wife nearly lost her balance.

When Santi was about to throw the chopper in her direction, she pleaded with her in a tremulous voice, "No, don't kill me, O sister of mine!" And she was pushed up against the wall. Slicing off a big hole in the *salwar* of Maghar's wife, the chopper fell upon the pillar in the front, piercing it as deep as four fingers.

With her fear-stricken eyes, when Santi saw the ashen-pale, bloodless face of Maghar's wife and the chopper hanging off the wall, all her brutal strength was drained away. She had not set eyes upon such a fear-stricken, pure and innocent face ever. She couldn't get herself to lay her hands on the chopper again. It was as though all her energy had been sapped out of her body; her legs began to tremble and she found it hard to stand on her two feet. Reclining against the wall, she managed to steady herself with a great difficulty.

The very next moment, Santi felt giddy, as though she was losing consciousness, and in that state of giddiness, each and every word in someone's tremulous voice was stabbing into her heart.

"If you're so miserable because of me, O sister of mine! ...then I must go...O sister! What would you get by killing someone like me who is already half dead! ...You think, I deliberately call your 'master' here and offer him drinks? What do you know, sister, that I'm a 'paid for commodity.' I sit or stand wherever my 'master' asks me to – I've no will of my own! ...Sister, I'm nothing more than dirt. These men have scraped my skin with their teeth..."

"That time, it was my love for life that got the better of me. But what am I going to get out of this world? It's much better to die at your hands than allow these dogs to flay my skin alive! ...Take this chopper, come and kill me — Why don't you kill me?"

And Santi had lost her consciousness.

The third day after this incident when people heard that Maghar's wife had run away somewhere, lying upon *manji*, distraught, Santi was talking all to herself as though she had lost her head:

"O you sinner, Santiye! You didn't even ask her who she was? ...Did she have someone she could depend on and be assured of two square meals a day? ...O sinner! Where'll she go now? ...O Santiye! Both the worlds are lost on you...How'd you be redeemed now? ..."

Ambo

At the time of entering the compartment, when that plump woman hit the floor with a *beri* stick she held in her hand, its sound sent a sudden tremor through Surjit's body. Appraising that woman, her eyes nearly popped out as though she had set them upon something rather bizarre. Standing in the middle of the compartment, that woman stared at the wooden seats in such a manner as if she had come prepared to beat someone up, and now stood looking for him.

"Ambo, there is hardly any place to sit," said another woman, who appeared to be married and was standing right behind her.

Lashing the stick out against the floor, again, Ambo spoke with a real authority, "Don't you worry about that! God be thanked, there're plenty of seats here. Now just look at this lady! There is so much of space next to her."

And with these words that woman, Ambo, stepped forward and slumped down into the little space between Surjit and a young man sitting next to her, edging both out as she squeezed herself in.

"*Uyee!*...My hand." Surjit nearly screamed.

Resting her hand upon the stick, first that woman twisted around to look at Surjit in bewilderment but then seeing her press her hand, she burst into a spontaneous laughter. Holding Surjit's wrist in her hand very gingerly and pressing it gently, she said, "*Bibi*, I hope you haven't sprained your wrist." On hearing this, the women sitting around her also burst out laughing. Ambo's lady-in-the-waiting, the one who had followed her into the compartment, laughed and said, "Ambo, these days, boys and girls are so very delicate. They appear to be made of butter paper. Just float around in the wind. I won't be surprised if the wrist has actually been sprained. It is only to be expected."

"Except the burnt-out ash, what's there inside them?" hollered Ambo, almost in the manner of a heifer, "O you fool, they eat nothing but *Dalda ghee* and the tea they drink is enough to make one vomit! So how do you expect them to be healthy?"

Though that woman had not felt embarrassed in the least about using the word 'vomit,' Surjit had definitely begun to feel the churning inside her. Leaving her hand to just hang loosely about, she started peering out of the window.

"Now just look at this *bibi*," Ambo laughed and said, "She'd also claim to be as young as anyone else…Just a little weight her hand had to take, and she screamed as if she had fractured her arm or leg!"

And then she broke into a loud guffaw. The other women, who were with her, also started laughing. But their laughter had none of the rumbling sounds that resonated in Ambo's laughter. It was almost as if they hadn't quite approved of laughing at this well turned out, educated woman.

Beads of perspiration appeared on Surjit's forehead. Fairly reticent by nature, hearing Ambo jabber away, she had now retreated into a sullen silence. In the city, she had seen so many *jat* women but her kind she hadn't ever had a chance to meet. As she was extremely self-conscious, her breathing, too, had slowed down considerably. Looking in, she turned up her nose a little and then again, started peering out of the window. It appeared as though Ambo's thick spread had left her body rather hamstrung, especially after all this pushing and jostling. But she just didn't have the courage to speak up against such a woman.

Ambo's companions had settled down on the floor, right

in front of her. And now Ambo was sitting like a queen, holding the stick in both the hands, her heavy waist protruding. Delicately embroidered, muslin, *chunni* lay casually upon her shoulder, leaving half of her head uncovered. With a broad forehead, an equally broad face and a neck as thick as that of a bull, she really looked to be their gang-leader.

"Santo, last year, our Jalora somehow happened to go to town," Ambo set the ball rolling, stealing a glance towards Surjit.

"Which Jalora? Namho's uncle-in-law?" queried Santo.

"O you fool, of course, the same! The wicked one who gallivants around just like a flying snake," as Santo, another middle-aged woman sitting behind her, explained it to her, all of them fell out laughing. Ambo picked up the loose threads, once again.

"He said, 'I was walking towards the district courts in Bathinda when I saw a girl peddling down the road. Now I hadn't ever seen a girl ride a bicycle.'..."

"That stupid fellow must be just gassing around! The whole day long, he does nothing but roam the streets of various towns and yet he pretends, he hasn't seen a girl ride a bicycle!" wondered Santo with a scowl

"Why bother about that? You just listen to the story," is how Ambo advised Santo, casting yet another squinted glance towards Surjit and both broke into a suppressed laughter.

Surjit had come to know of their laughter. She felt a sudden stab of pain deep inside, and her hand started aching all over again. Almost as a reflex, pulling her hand out of the window, she started pressing it for comfort.

Why, *bibi*, is it aching still?" asked Ambo in a gentle but mocking tone, stroking Surjit's back. But Surjit had begun to break into a cold sweat.

"Now come on, girlie! Won't her hand hurt? It's been crushed under the road-roller, after all."

And all of them burst out laughing, all over again.

"He says, 'When that girl came closer to me…' And he had described her to be somewhat like this one, as thin as a reed…" said Ambo, twisting things around just to drag Surjit into the conversation, 'all the books lying in her cycle basket fell off.' He says, 'I called out to her and she twisted around to look back and slowed down her bicycle. But for a long time, she didn't get off the bicycle. And standing there, I kept wondering why she was taking such a long time to get off. When she got closer to the books, first she stared at the books and then, me. I kept wondering why she isn't picking up the books? There was a little distance between us. So I kept inching closer to her. I asked her *'Bibi,* are these your books?' She nodded her head but didn't say a word. I asked in surprise, 'If these are yours, then why don't you pick them up?' When I asked her this question, she made a face akin to that of a kid-lamb (as it is, it wasn't like that of a lion) and meowing like a cat, she tells me, *'Babaji,* will you pick up these books for me?' I don't know what she meant when she repeatedly kept saying something like 'police,' 'police.' Of course, it made no sense to me. I thought to myself why can't she pick up her own books? Then it occurred to me that, being the daughter of rich parents, she perhaps thinks it beneath her dignity to do her work. I collected the books and handed them over to her. She put all the books on the carrier behind her seat and after saying something like 'Fank you,' 'Fank you' she left. I thought to myself, who knows, the shrewd one might have flung an abuse or two. She dragged the bicycle for some distance, but when she was about to ride it, she couldn't even manage to lift her leg. For quite some time, she kept struggling with it. When she finally made a bid to climb by hopping on to it, the seams of her *kurta* split. That is when I understood why she had asked me to lift her books. So tightly was her *kurta* stitched right down to her knees that she couldn't have possibly bent down to lift her books. When it all sank into me, I nearly doubled over with laughter and kept repeating. 'To hell with such children!' …." Now that's the kind of story he narrated about the city-girls. I don't know how much of it was really true or whether it was all cooked up. He must have added things on his own. Quite a devil he is…" Ambo had barely finished narrating the story, when her companions blew it all up into a raucous laughter.

So completely engrossed was she in listening to Ambo's story that Surjit didn't even realise when the train steamed off or when it rushed passed the *kothas* on the way. Though somewhat annoyed over this blatantly candid manner in which Ambo was talking, Surjit had begun to relish it as well.

The entire compartment was packed with men, but that didn't seem to deter her in any way. Blissfully unaware of everyone around, she was busy talking so animatedly as though she was holding an open court in her own backyard. And this was something that seemed to appeal to Surjit as much as it revolted her. It was within a span of minutes that she had both liked and disliked, her authoritative voice, raucous laughter, devil-may-care attitude and her jovial nature, several times over. 'What kind of a woman is she?' It was while musing over Ambo in this manner that Surjit had suddenly been plunged into strange thoughts about herself.

First of all, her mind went back to the incident that had happened yesterday morning. While leaving for school, she had hardly boarded the train when another middle-aged teacher from the same school had come and sat himself next to her. Until the end of the journey, he had kept talking to her on one pretext or the other. So useless were the inanities he got into that responding to him had left her both tired and angry. And yet she hadn't been able to muster as much courage as was needed for not responding to any of his queries.

When she had enrolled herself for the basic course, she would often get to hear abuses couched in the vulgar songs sung by the young louts idling around the street corners. So scared was she of them that she wouldn't even dream of going to the institute on her own, or return from there alone. All the time she would be scared that any one of them might just start teasing her. That is why, even when accompanied by her friends, she would be on her guards while going past them. That time, she didn't fear older men so much. But after yesterday's incident, she had begun to fear men of all ages. She felt as though someone or the other was chasing her around all the time. And that someone was the one who appeared more like a giant, had no specific age and would sometimes become a young lad, a middle-aged person or an old man. Whenever she heard the footfalls of someone walking close on her heels, she would suddenly turn around with such trepidation as though that person was going to gobble her up.

"... These days, girls are very brainy, but they go around wearing such tight fitting, skin-hugging, *kurtas* and pyjamas that almost make them look like she-rats." Ambo hadn't lost the thread of her conversation and her audience was still listening and laughing just as before.

" The grand-daughter of our village *zaildaar* came to stay with him. It was some four months ago. They said that she was in some big school, somewhere in Chandigarh. O you fool! It must be some college or something. Wearing high-heeled sandals, specks on her eyes and her head uncovered, she used to go around preening herself."

"One day, while she happened to be sitting on a chair, someone set *zaildaar's* calf loose in the courtyard. Coming closer, the calf gave her half a kick with its rear hooves. And she, along with the chair, rolled down on the ground like a rotund pitcher. And near the wrist, her arm split open like a carrot. When I heard about it, I cursed the girl with all my heart. I said, even the glass bangles don't get smashed so easily. Now look at this! The girls are so fragile these days. We, too, had our bodies, after all... Now this perhaps happened in 93, I was taking the buffaloes for water. One of our healthier she-calves ran off with her iron chain. I caught hold of her chain while she was running away. I didn't let her go across the field. Putting my foot on the chain, I bound her down in such a manner that she almost started gasping for breath, her tongue lolling out…."

"Ambo, you're really unbeatable. I remember, you had no problems polishing off a kilo and a half of pudding at one go, " said Santo, with a smile.

"Those times were really different. Now the body is simply bloated, though it has nothing inside it. But still I'm much better off than these silly fools!" While speaking these words, Ambo first smiled and looked at Surjit and then asked her in a very humble tone, "O daughter of mine! Is your hand still hurting you?"

And, once again, they all broke into laughter, Ambo openly and the others muffling theirs.

But this time round, Surjit was not offended by their laughter. Her hand was not hurting any more. Even Ambo's protruding waistline stuck in her side appeared to radiate warmth to her. Now she almost yearned to listen more and more of her stories, and each time they broke into a loud laughter, a quiet smile suffused her face as well.

"O daughter of mine! You shouldn't really feel bad about the behaviour of likes of us – simple *jats*, that what we are. A few days' fair is what this life is, so why not laugh our way through it….?" said Ambo, patting Surjit's back gently, once again.

"No one really minds it, *ji*… " It was as though these words had escaped her lips involuntarily or perhaps the smile on her face had emboldened her somewhat.

"Well said! Well said!….That's why we often say that girls, these days, don't lack intelligence but health. It's their bodies, not minds, which are like stuffed camels. In our times, it was only body and nothing else as our minds were no better than those of the animals…." And stroking Surjit's back, Ambo started laughing, once again.

"What is one going to do with the mind alone?" Surjit spoke again.

"No child, mind is really a great blessing…."

Then suddenly the compartment broke into pell-mell confusion. People were taking their luggage off the wooden slabs. They were trying to get their brood together. The train had slowed down considerably. And within less than a minute, it came to a halt. A thick set, *jat,* standing in the doorway, had several large bundles blocking the way. There was a young man in front of him. It took him quite some time to get off the train. Then the *jat* took his own time, handing the bundles over to him. Ambo and her companions were right behind him. For some time, Ambo simply kept glaring at the *jat* but then she could bear it no longer.

"*Weh, bhai,* will you let anyone else also to get off or no?" asked Ambo in her stentorian voice.

While handing in the third bundle, the *jat* suddenly turned around and spoke rather sharply, "Why are you in such a hurry? Do you have to attend a hearing in the court?"

"Do you want us to wait here until the evening? Will you cook some rice and offer it to us, then?"

"Old woman, but look at the way she speaks?" Getting edgier, the *jat* looked at Ambo.

"Exactly the way you speak."

"Now this is really the limit!…Such a shrew…"

"Another word and I'll break your jaw with this stick — How dare you call me a shrew? …."

And Ambo actually lifted her stick up. Surjit was standing right behind her. She couldn't help laughing.

The expression in the *jats'* eyes had changed all of a sudden. Hurriedly removing the remaining two bundles, he got off himself and started muttering under his breath.

"They behave as if their father has bought the train for a price!" screamed Ambo, looking at him with a squinted eye as she struck the whip, once again, on the platform. Beads of sweat had appeared on the *jats* forehead and he was sinking within. He couldn't get himself to utter a word, again.

After disembarking from the train, Surjit looked at Ambo's broad face again, and her soft, delicate features were imprinted upon her mind. When she looked towards Ambo again, her head bowed a little as if in reverence.

And now when she walked towards the gate, her neck was straight as ramrod and her gait as sharp and crisp as Ambo's voice. Her legs were not shaking like the cane-sticks anymore, and she wasn't in the least afraid of the men walking by her side.

Bonding

On disembarking from the train, a lady was simply looking around, perplexed. Bantu squinted at her. (As his vision had
deteriorated, he was not able to recognise a person from a distance). On coming closer, he felt as though it was Jai Kaur.

"Who is it?"

"I'm Jai Kaur."

"How come you're here?"

And that very moment, Bantu broke into a warm smile.
First, Jai Kaur became somewhat self-conscious and then said, "I
had gone to town. The elder daughter-in-law is admitted to a
hospital there."

"Is she all right?"

"Yes, she's going to have a baby."

"Come, let's go, then."

Jai Kaur could not think of anything to say. She was in a
dilemma. The sun had already set and by the time she got to the
village, it would anyway be quite late for the meals. Somehow, no
third person had got off the train. And the train, too, never used to
chug in so late, it would always come in well before sundown but
today, it had really been late, a good deal. It did occur to her once
that she should spend the night at her nephew's house, but she
had to return by the next train, the following day, in the afternoon.
Thinking it over for a minute, she peered at Bantu, standing in
front of her. There was a strange glow in his eyes, and in his
demeanour, a rare simplicity.

"All right, then. Let's go!" said Jai Kaur, firming up her
mind.

As Bantu cut a long stride, the bundle of vegetables rest-

ing upon his head became somewhat unsteady. Holding it in place
with both his hands, he made a sound as though he were trying to
tame a wild heifer. Later, he mumbled something to himself and
started smiling on his own.

"So Jai Kaure, what's new?" As they hit the road, Bantu
started the conversation in a genial manner, "Is your family all
right?"

"It's all Guru's grace."

"So be it. So be it."

And Bantu cleared his throat. Looking towards his right
and left, when his eyes caught the crimson radiance of the setting
sun, he felt a deep sense of joy inside. Seeing that the split-ear of
the millet seed was still ablaze in the fields, he lowered his eyes,
once again.

There was such an eerie silence all around that even the
sparrows could hear their footfalls. Perched among the trees lined
on either side of the road, when the sparrows started twittering, it
appeared as if their noise would sunder the sky apart. And when
the sparrows stopped twittering, the silence descended all over
again. For quite some distance, Bantu kept walking, hearing the
footfalls of Jai Kaur behind him. This sound was music to his ears,
almost like the melody of a drum and cymbals in the *gurudwara*...

"Jai Kaure, haven't we met after several years...?"

"Yes!" It was almost as if Jai Kaur had responded in a
trembling voice. "Weren't you with your nephew in Rajasthan for
six-seven years?"

"Yes."

Looking up at Bantu, Jai Kaur felt a shiver run through
her body. He had suddenly stopped and was staring back, dusting the sand off his *jutti*. His eyes were ablaze with the crimson
colour of the setting sun. But seeing his salt-and-pepper beard,
Jai Kaur felt somewhat reassured...Now she had nothing to fear
or feel shy about. Until now, it hadn't really dawned on her that
Bantu had grown much older. Picking up his stride again, Bantu
laughed all to himself. Now when the distance between them was

no more than five yards, Jai Kaur could size him up from head to toe. Bantu's calf-muscles had shrunk to the size of a stick. And flesh around his neck lay sagging. His back had developed a pronounced hump. And his shoulder blades had started jutting out like the horns of a buffalo-calf. His clothes were reeking of grime and sweat. And suddenly, another Bantu came and stood before Jai Kaur's eyes....This Bantu's forehead was as majestic as that of a monarch. He was tall and statuesque, had a muscular body and amorous eyes with a strange glow, difficult to bear. This very Bantu....

This thought made Jai Kaur tremble, again. Scared, she had started looking at Bantu from the corner of her eye. But the very next moment, her lips broke into a quiet smile.

"You look rather weak?" This time, Jai Kaur asked him in a soft voice, full of compassion, "Have you been ailing or something?"

Bantu took a deep sigh and said, "Jai Kaure...now you should not ask anything about it."

"Don't get so disheartened," Jai Kaur consoled him, "Everyone has to face problems. After all, it's domestic life, more of a web, really."

"I agree. It's a web, Jai Kaure, but the times are so bad that no one bothers for anyone now. Tell me, is this my age to be knocking around like this? .... It's been ten years now since I gave away all the property to my sons. Their looks have changed, and they don't bother for me at all. Both the daughters-in-law are so bad, they say, why not flay this old man's skin alive. What good is he, otherwise? No one gives food on time or water for my bath. No one does my washing, no nothing! ...Why blame anyone? You suffer your own *karmas*, after all, Jai Kaure!"

Suddenly, Jai Kaur felt as though Bantu was a small child who, having been beaten up at home, was complaining now.

"Never mind. One shouldn't get so upset." Jai Kaur spoke in a firm voice this time, "Just look at people like me who have no home, so to say. As it is, God never listened to me all through life.

Besides, I had to depend upon my nephews — with brothers, it's very different. Every living being is unhappy, you see. As they say, 'Nanak, suffering is the fate of all souls in this world.' No one can control the destiny. It's what you sow that you ultimately reap. As they say, '*Karma* is a field, you'll reap what you seed.'"

While Jai Kaur was talking, Bantu felt somewhat reassured. It was the kind of reassurance that an unhappy person experience only when he sees another of his kind; in a way much more than that, for he had some kind of a 'deep bonding' with Jai Kaur.

Bantu looked towards the left. The crimson colour of the setting sun was no longer visible now. In the clear, open sky, the stars had begun to peep out at places. As there was no breeze, it had become rather humid. And now the sounds of the cattle-herds could also not be heard anymore. The dusty track had become much narrower now. Very confidently, Jai Kaur was bringing up the rear. Her sonorous voice, ageing features on her milk-white complexion, impressive, broad forehead and skin that hadn't wizened still. (She had retained that magnetic pull, which women are often known to possess). He had been admiring her all to himself and now simply wanted to stand by and stare at her.

"Jai Kaure, this is our field." Rubbing his feet against his *jutti* and dusting the sand off it, he had stopped again and was pointing towards the thick, cotton field to his right, "This time round, we've sown more than five acres — right up to that *tahli* tree in the front."

Jai Kaur stopped all of a sudden. She was out of breath, as her heartbeat had quickened. (It was the same *tahli* under which Bantu had once accosted her and without the least hesitation had grabbed her arm, nearly thirty years ago... Scared only for a-split-second, Jai Kaur had then felt that Bantu should keep holding her arm in this manner...). Jai Kaur had started trembling. On the pretext of dusting sand off his *jutti*, Bantu hadn't cut another stride and now stood staring at her, wide-eyed. Meeting his eyes once or twice, Jai Kaur lowered her gaze, again. Now dead-

scared of Bantu, she felt that his wizened face looked quite dreadful.

"And right next to the *tahli*, it's maize." Bantu spoke as
though he was teasing her, "I had told them to sow cotton there as
well. But you know who bothers for the 'old blokes' like us. They
do what they feel like."

"That's right. That's right."

"Jai Kaure, my *bapu* was going to sell this *tahli* at the
time of my marriage. But I dug my heels in and said, 'Do what you
have to, mortgage the land or whatever, but I won't let you sell
this *tahli* at any cost.'"

Again, strange tremors had run through Jai Kaur's body.
Bantu was insisting upon dragging *tahli* into the conversation, time
and again. Now when they turned around, Jai Kaur slowed down
and fell behind him by twenty yards or so. Bantu could no longer
hear Jai Kaur's footfalls. He suddenly paused in the middle of his
sentence and started looking at her.

"Come along, come along, now. We've almost made it."
Bantu said, cheering her up, "There lies the village. Hardly any
distance now."

Jai Kaur looked ahead. The village was no more than half
a mile now. She picked her stride and fell in step with Bantu.

"Jai Kaure, ever since your *bharjai* died, I feel as though
I'm only breathing and not living."

Bantu stressed 'your *bharjai*' in a manner that made Jai
Kaur break into a quiet smile.

"Jai Kaure!" Bantu spoke again, "It's just a question of
age. When 'we' were young, 'we' never ever remembered God!
And now it seems as if 'we' are a burden on this earth. And it'd
be much better if 'we' were to die. But bloody death is something
that isn't really granted when it's sought…"

"*Weh,* why do you think of death," Jai Kaur said, "You
should wait until your grandsons are married off. You shouldn't
go before you've played with your great grandsons. Besides, as
they say, unless the great grandsons touch your head, you don't

get salvation."

On hearing Jai Kaur's words, Bantu became somewhat reflective, It was as though he wanted to live and die, the very same moment.

"You're right in away. But what'll I get by dragging myself on my knees, really? Who is bothered about salvation, anyway? This is no life, really. Almost the entire family treats me as if I were no more than a dog. No one is happy serving me a crumb even."

And Jai Kaur felt that Bantu was saying the right thing. Suddenly she felt as close to Bantu as she had felt some thirty years ago, when both were 'alike,' young and unmarried. Even today, they were 'alike' — always looking towards other people's hands, expecting to be served. For twenty years, she had been longing for a child, but no *devi-devta* or *peer-fakir* had shown any mercy upon her. Finally, her husband's sudden death had put an end to all her expectations. And now for the past seven years, she had been dividing her time between her parents-in-law and her parents. Again, she would go and squat at the door of her nephews. For her daily bread and butter, she really had to slave it out for one and all!...

"Jai Kaure, it's only for the sake of the slavery of these sons and grandsons that you lump so much. Otherwise, they are the kinds who would not only abuse you seven hundred times over but also throw you out of the house — they treat you no better than a dog, really..." While narrating his story, Bantu was slowly slipping into his earlier mood.

"Jai Kaure, this is no existence, really! When no one is even going to think of you once you're gone, what kind of death is it? For a lonely person, death is also a curse, really!"

Bantu went on talking but Jai Kaur was no longer paying much heed to him. She was looking at the earthen lamps burning far into the village, which appeared to her more like the flames rising from the cremation ground.

Turning around, she looked at Bantu. His rickety, thin legs had become invisible in the darkness. His thin frame was trembling, as it were. Jai Kaur was suddenly overwhelmed with compassion for him.

"All right, I'll take the outer road, then!" She told Bantu, "Don't get upset. Why not smile as long as we live. No one is really going to look after us better if we start cribbing."

"That's rather well said. Very well said." With these words, Bantu turned into his street.

The Topmost Bough

In a way, it was the city's most God-forsaken road. In the daytime, hardly anyone would go along that way, but in the mornings and afternoons, it really would be in great demand, especially when the boys and girls of the college would pass from there, dressed up in their fineries. All places are good, but only because of their respective people! It was during this short-lived ebullience that the road would often come alive. Close to this road, in a ramshackle *basti,* dating back to the times of Maharaja Ranjit Singh, lived he along with his old mother in a run-down shanty.

All the college going boys and girls were fairly attractive but of them all, he liked the thin, golden-wheat complexioned girl the most. Often while crossing the first bend in the road, she would cast a very natural look towards the door of their house. Small but neatly arranged things in their respective places would inevitably attract her attention, as much as they did anyone else's. There must have been magic in the hands of Basant's mother that she had transformed this centuries-old shanty into a beautiful home. But slowly, it was something else that had begun to engage her attention. Now almost everyday, as soon as she reached near the bend, lifting her head, she would cast a glance towards the door. Basant felt that she would occasionally flash a smile at him as well.

After a few days, Basant, too, started looking spruced up, very much like the neat things of the well-arranged house. Now he wouldn't be seen dressed as a ruffian the way he used to be earlier. Having a daily bath, combing his hair and wearing neat clothes were now among his regular habits. So much so that he had begun to look rather handsome even to his own mother.

"Banti, my son, you seem to have changed somewhat now…" One day, his mother told him very hesitantly, as she handed him a glass of tea. But after a while, she had started cursing herself, "What if my son falls under the influence of my own evil eye!"

He just laughed and fell silent. 'But he really has changed,' as this thought swept over his mother, her heartbeat quickened with delight. A sudden tidal wave that often rises in an evenly flowing river of life has the power to wash over the banks as well.

Basant was barely five years old when his father died. His mother brought him up by washing other people's dishes. He was in class five when his mother fell ill and could not get up from bed for close to two months. Removed from the school, he was sent to a rich man's house to work as a domestic. His mother did recover and though she was still in a position to work as much as she needed to feed herself, her age didn't allow her to bear the reproaches of the people any longer. So thereafter, Basant washed the dishes, did baby-sitting, filled the water, scoured the huge vessels of the *halwais*, fetched and carried the milk, sold peanuts and that's how he spent the first twenty years of his life.

Now for the past two years, he had been working in a leather factory. Initially, for a few days, he had found it extremely difficult to stand the smell of the hide but then it had ceased to matter. Even now, when at night, he occasionally dreamt of that golden-wheat complexioned girl or carved her well-cut, sharp features out of the irradiating glow of the stars, the next morning, while walking towards the main gate of the factory, the revolting smell of the hide and the bones would hit his nostrils all over again. Scared of the stench, if someone were to run away, he probably would have no place to live in this world – as almost everywhere around there was stink of one kind or another – so where could he go, really? The heavy noise of the machines would make him forget almost everything.

For about ten to twelve hours a day, he had to carry

leather, shavings of *keekar* and more such rubbish around. Occasionally, he had to put in three-four hours of extra work as well. But now he would not feel much tired. Every day, a new life would start surging up within him and that girl, too, would top it with her own sparkling presence, sending waves of exhilaration through him as he went around. Earlier whenever the owner of the factory visited in his car, seeing his blood-shot eyes, he used to feel scared but now it spurred him on to do more work. Sometimes, the owner would appreciate his work as well — for it was work, not complexion that he liked more – and now he had really started doing a good job.

Even that girl had begun to like Basant somewhat – just the way anything familiar, after a while, with which we have had some association, begins to appeal to us. From near the bend in the road when she looked, Basant would be sitting upon his *manji*, holding a glass of tea in hand. Sometimes, she really seemed to respond rather well to his sharp features, impressive height and neat clothes; certainly much more than those of the other boys from her college. And what she really liked the most was the sweet, innocent expression in his eyes, which was so hard to come by in others. It was almost as if his eyes shone with some inexplicable desire, a yearning or a hunger. While crossing the bend, so many times would she adjust the *pallu* of her *saree*, pressing the pile of books harder against her bosom. And as she passed by their door, her gait would become sprightlier and face suddenly aglow with the flush of dawn, radiating a very different look in her eyes. A strong desire to talk to her simmering inside him, Basant would peer into her eyes, often forgetting to sip tea from the glass, next to his lips. Even when he went out, sometimes, he couldn't get himself to call out to her.

Basant's mother was quite a sensible woman. Almost everyday, she would notice how both of them stared at each other, but seeing this, she would simply smile, lowering her eyes almost instantly. Her wrinkled up hands would break into tremors. Thinking something over to herself, she would sigh rather deeply and cast the same kind of look at Basant that a gardener often gives to a young plant, throbbing with the intense desire for fruition without actually coming into it.

Saddened by her thoughts, one day, his mother said:

"Son, the sensible birds don't make nests upon the topmost boughs, for the fear of rain and storm is always greater there." It was almost as she was trying to instil into him centuries-old wisdom.

But that young traveller, who was searching for newer paths and so walked a few inches above the ground, simply went his way, his feet staggering somewhat, though.

One afternoon, he was standing close to the trough used for washing the hide, his hand resting upon the tap. Suddenly, he heard roar of the car engine; the owner had come. Today, a young girl had accompanied him. Basant looked at her very carefully, several times over, and darkness fell over his eyes. His legs began to tremble. She was the same college-going, golden-complexioned girl. Unable to keep standing there any more, he sat down with the support of the water pipe. While sitting, he peered, sneaking a look through the crevice of his arm covering his face; the owner and that girl had come much closer.

"What's the matter, *bai*? Why are you sitting like this?" asked the owner somewhat angrily.

"*Ji*, I've a headache." By telling a lie as big as his pain, he tried to put a lid over the heart overflowing underneath.

"If you've a headache, why don't you take leave and go home? Why at our cost must you. ..." And muttering in this manner, the owner went on ahead. It was as if all the senses of Basant had taken leave of him.

Both of them had walked on ahead.

Slowly, coming into himself, he looked at his undershirt and underwear, stained with the colour of the shavings, and also looked at the dirt and grime staining different parts of his body. Seeing all this made him feel so giddy that, for quite some time, he didn't even realise where he was sitting. After a long time, when he recovered his senses, the car was still there. Getting up from there, he went and lay down in the quarter of Ratta, the watchman.

In the evening, while leaving, when he queried one of his fellow workers, he told him that she was the owner's daughter who had come to the factory, the first time ever. On returning home, he didn't have anything to eat. He gave his mother the same excuse of a headache. The next morning when he got up, his head was heavy and eyes red with sleeplessness. Wearing the same set of crumpled, old clothes, he sat down to drink his cup of tea. When he saw the same girl coming in, he didn't even look towards the door. Coming closer, she gave him a squinted look and stepped up her pace. Picking up his lunch box, Basant, too, followed her. Earlier also, many a time, he had followed her in this manner and as he got closer, she would slow down, bringing certain springiness into her gait. But today, seeing him follow her, she almost wanted to take to her heels. He, too picked up his stride but this time when the girl turned around to look back, there was no affection, only a strange fear in her eyes. Walking apace, she crossed the gate of the college in such a tearing hurry as though a *jinni* was trailing her.

He didn't turn towards the factory, and by the time he looked up, he had reached the bus-stand, where he stopped. Thinking something over, he decided to turn back and proceed to the factory. By the time he reached there, the *munshi* had already marked him absent. Grabbing hold of the *munshi's* throat, he started pressing it, almost like a man possessed, so hard that his eyes nearly popped out. His fellow workers jumped in to disengage him and everyone was surprised, wondering what had really happened to him.

Then in that very state, he came out of the factory. By the time, he had returned home, it was well past midnight. The full moon was on a decline towards the west and a grey cloud towards its left was drifting away, slowly.

"Banti, you've been out so late, today…" His mother left the sentence unfinished when she realised that he was dead-drunk.

He would never return home drunk and, that too, so late.

His mother nearly let out a scream.

"What have you done, my son? The only prop of my old age – it'll spell total darkness for me, O my son...." And with a corner of her *chunni,* she started wiping the tears off her deep-set, aged eyes.

"Hanh, Maa! The darkness will...re...ally sp...re ...ad...the dark... ness! Do...you...see...that...big...cloud, it'll... eclipse... the... moon... and... the... dark... ness...will...spread." Pointing towards the moon, he first fell out laughing like a man crazed and then slumped on to the *manji.*

And passing over the moon, the grey cloud had already eclipsed it, spreading the darkness all around. Lying stock-still, he felt as though, sitting by his side, his mother was saying,

"Son, the sensible birds don't ever build their nests upon the topmost boughs. The fear of rain and storm is always greater there." The same centuries-old wisdom that she always carried around with her.

Darkness lay suffusing his entire being.

In My Own Hand

I'm quite sure, the moment you hear my name you would be reminded of that old woman and whatever she is believed to have said during the fair. They say, once when an old woman lost her son during a fair, she went around crying herself hoarse. She must have searched through the bowels of earth seven times over before naming her son as — Chand Singh. When she was busy calling out his name in desperation, some mischief-maker like myself started trailing her, poking fun at her. It so happened that after some time, the old woman's Chand Singh showed up in all his characteristic brilliance. Blind in one eye, lame in one leg, the upper two teeth missing and the body, all cracked and chipped. It seemed as though after carving him out, God had put him to dry. When he had dried up, God was dismayed seeing his own creation. So in a fit of anger, He gave him such a stinging blow that all those parts of poor Chand Singh's body that had already dried up, cracked like the slender *kareer* wood. But as far as the old woman was concerned, he was her *Id ka Chand!* She asked him repeatedly, 'O my son, where were you?' But for more than an hour, or so, Chand Singh kept twisting his neck around, trying to straighten his jaw. How could the poor fellow have responded, his jaw still askew? The die-hard tease, who was following her around, couldn't hold himself back and said, '*Mai,* so this is your Chand Singh?' Seeing a glint of mischief in his eyes, the old woman turned livid. So she snapped back, 'Why, *bhai,* you want to fix up an alliance with him?' The tease was more than a patch on her.

He was not the one to be outwitted so easily. He laughed

and said, 'O bloody woman, you talk of an alliance, I don't give a damn to him.'

So our innocent, simple-minded mother, too, named me 'Puran Chand!' In a way God treated me in a manner no different from the one in which he had treated Chand Singh. First, He used that soil as a material for shaping me that had been rotting away in the cesspool for over twenty years. And when he sat down to sculpt me out, who knows what went wrong with him. Whether he had had too much of opium or had fought with his wife, that son of his father just didn't bother about anything, he simply fixed up the arms or the legs wherever he could find a place to fit them in. He twisted the jaw at places and made one shoulder higher than the other.

What is, indeed, surprising is that God was not the only one to have worked against me. That two-penny, rotten woman, who is popularly known as *Vidh Mata,* too, had decided to act as high and mighty, especially when my turn came. She must have thought that now that she had the pen in her hand, she must spill all her venom on Puran Chand. She must have fought with her family members over her grandfather's property or something. Perhaps it was her husband who had given her a good thrashing. Whatever it was, she had apparently decided to take it all out on me.

So, Sir, this is what happened with me in the other world. Now you listen to the story of this mortal world.

Yes sir, 'your highness' incarnated into this world on the fourth day of Baisakh in the year nineteen hundred and nineteen in the early hours of a Sunday. My maternal grandmother used to tell us that emboldened by my 'incarnation,' my mother had returned to the grinding stone on the fifth or the seventh day after 'our' birth. Father of mine had thrown his coffers open. Leaping through the air he had proclaimed, "So friends, today 'we,' too, can count ourselves among the settled ones. Now 'we' don't care a damn for anything in the world!" If on one hand, the *shahzada* had his future written in golden letters, on the other, he brought along the death warrants for several of his near and dear ones, too. Within the first fortnight or so, mother gave up the ghost. Then, by God's grace, within five years or so, the other relatives, too, were despatched. Everyone boarded the Bombay mail, long distance passes in their pockets. Like a lame goat's tail, *shahzada* was the only one left.

Come to think of it, a five-year old *shahzada* became the sovereign ruler of all the three worlds. Whenever hunger gnawed at my innards, I would grab three or four *rotis* from wherever 'we' could and that was that. And often I dropped off to sleep wherever the night fell. This is how inhabitants of different villages and cities managed to indulge their compassion. So after playing the role of a messiah, I finally decided to make Jaito, a small town, my home.

Now listen to the next part of the story. Sir my age must have been close to seven years then, and I was given to roaming around freely in Shah's street when *Vidh Mata's* writ began to tear itself apart. Seth Girdhari Lal's eyes fell upon me. Being a typical businessman, he made quick calculations and figured out that at this price, it wouldn't be a bad bargain at all. From then on, this 'wandering saint' set up his *dera* there. As they agreed to provide me everything, food and clothing included, so I accepted it in the name of God's will. I would do just about everything I was asked to. Now, nothing of this kind could have possibly worn out different parts of my body. Not that I really was expected to oil an entire horse-cart. All I had to do was to scour a few dishes, tend to the children and keep the place clean as far as possible.

For full ten years, Sir, Puran Chand had a whale of a time. People thought that I was a fool, offering myself up for exploitation. Had I been working for someone else, I would have made a neat pile. But friends, that was the time I was really riding a high horse. So how could I have listened to anyone? I haven't known a man more shrewd than the Chaudhary. Every time he saw me malingering, he would quietly pull his shoe off and start thrashing me. That did the trick just as well.

So this is how ten, twelve years simply went rushing by.

And then came the youth, swishing and hissing like a darkening storm! Punnu became Puran Chand, once again a full moon! ...Now the moment you hear this bit about such an animal as myself stepping into youth, you'd probably laugh yourself into stitches. But youth, as you know, is something that the young ones of a donkey also experience. All said and done, I was, after all, a man's child!

Now listen to this one. Much before youth could actually set in, it had spent itself as well. It's rightly been said that when destruction is imminent, one starts doing things that are out of ordinary. Perhaps, our youth was to end as soon as it began; it blazed almost like a haystack on fire. *Janab*, the long and short of it is that I had begun to shun all work like plague. Now my heart was neither into scouring dishes nor into washing clothes. Now all my energy would go into dressing up in a pair of neat, well-washed clothes and styling my hair in such a manner that the puff remained intact. Earlier I used to feel shy, looking at a girl but now I just wanted to cast come-hither-glances at anyone or everyone. I went ahead and bought myself a kohl-stick, a comb, a looking glass and a bottle of scented hair oil.

After a few days, even our Shahs got to know that Puran Chand was on a different trip now, something that started giving them goose pimples. Anxious that I might end up creating some trouble at home, they decided to take me off the domestic chores and put me on duty at the shop. But being at the shop is something I hadn't ever liked, and when it's the call of youth, you know how it is. So, it didn't really take *santji* more than a few days to say 'Ram-Ram' for good and set off.

You know, the lone sparrows, such as I'm, are never really short of friends. One of my friends, Seeta, happened to be working for Hari, the *halwai*. He fixed me up there. Apart from the food and clothes I was to get, the work, too, was to my liking. Morning and evening, I was supposed to fetch milk from the village and run small errands around the shop. I started getting salary as well, fifteen rupees a month. So that was it. Now I would savour decent meals and spout all indecencies. In the flush of youth, if a man has money in his pocket, sky is the limit, really! We would see films, smoke 'lamp' cigarettes and spit over our shoulders. And kite flying is what we did all the time! It was as if day and night we slept on the bed of roses.

Then, one day, a very strange thing happened. My friend Seeta and I were waiting outside the ticket counter of a cinema hall. A well-dressed girl was standing in front of us — she appeared to be an educated person. Earlier I used to feel scared going closer to such girls, but now, I loved ogling at them. Besides, now I looked as respectable as anyone else. With my hair combed in style, bone-bleached, white dress shimmering and a leather *jutti* on my feet when I puffed at my cigarette from between my scissors-like fingers, then not even the queen's brother-in-law could dare disturb me

It was perhaps the first time ever that my self-esteem got a real battering. The moment that girl saw me, she wrinkled up her nose in such disgust as if she had suddenly walked into a pile of fresh dung. I thought to myself, 'Puran Chand, you may dress as well as you want or style your hair in whichever manner you wish, but all this is not going to change your God-given looks. You have neither the complexion nor the features. Then what do you pride yourself on, really? ...Well, some of your weaknesses might still be overlooked if you've a fat pocket – don't people do that all the time? I have seen hundreds who are as ugly as a heap of rubbish but go around flaunting wives, as beautiful as the moon itself. Don't they do it solely on the strength of their bulging pockets? O you fool! You don't even have enough in your pocket to be able to buy peanuts. So why give yourself airs, unnecessarily? So *janab,* you can imagine how bad I must have felt that time. Seeta kept pestering me to buy the tickets. But I said, 'Let's get back to the shop.' Finally, the poor fellow gave in and came back with me.

After returning to the shop, I couldn't get a wink of sleep all through the night. I was thrown into a real turmoil. I tried to reason it out with myself, 'You simpleton! Only if you had done good *karmas* could you have dreamt of being a rich man's son. What can possibly be done now?' My heart simply refused to listen to this logic. At that moment, all I wanted to do was to burst into tears. Again I told myself, 'Everyone has a place under the sun. Even those who never quite have enough to eat or dress all their lives are also human beings, after all. If they can go through life, uncomplainingly, why can't you?' Believe me, I had never ever given much thought to anything but that day, all kinds of thoughts kept floating up and down in my mind. Sometimes I would wonder, 'Do all these people who've good fun offer God a bribe before coming into this world? If they could enjoy a carefree existence, why couldn't God grant me the same?' But as you know, it's not for simpletons like us to figure such things out. I don't even know where God resides. Otherwise, I would have heaped all my anger over him and relieved myself. Finally, I simply decided to distract my mind in much the same way in which we often do it with a child. Do you think I had another choice?

From that time onwards, though I had stopped behaving in a snobbish manner, occasionally, my heart would go leaping out of itself. It was in such an inebriated state that once I happened to set my eyes upon Ratni, the one who used to wash the dishes. But she, too, glared at me so hard as though she had actually run into a heifer minutes before setting off towards her in-laws' house. Just come to think of it, she has nothing whatsoever to recommend herself. She has neither the face nor the forehead. Of course, the stomach that hangs about her does make her look like a woman. That day, again, I fell into deep thoughts. Throughout the day I kept thinking, 'Puran Chand, what kind of an existence is this that on seeing you, even such ugly ducklings turn up their noses in disgust?' But it was youth, after all. So after a few days, I was back to my old games, again.

Then one day, I got a feeling as though the daughter of Raju, the shoemaker, was showing some interest in me. I had never paid much attention to her earlier on. Somehow, the poor

girl was no better than I. Since I already had lost all other battles,
I decided to lock up my horns with her, finally. I thought to myself,
'Let me try out this *gur halwa* now.' One day, she was alone in
her hut. On the pretext of seeing the shoes, I just walked in. On
seeing me, she did show a sudden flush of joy but soon enough,
flashing her squinted eyes, she started counting the fingers of both
her hands in a somewhat suggestive manner. I did feel like giving
her a few tight slaps but then the thought that it might make matters worse stopped me short. It occurred to me, 'If such witches
have also started looking for ten rupee notes, then why blame
others?'

Now that was really the limit. I haven't cast my eyes on
any woman, since. No-one would have given a damn for a wastrel
like me, anyway. But the youth kept bubbling inside, turning all my
resolutions topsy-turvy. I would try and reason it out with myself,
but every time, my heart would overleap itself, very much like a
horse without reins. As if this wasn't enough, my friend, Seeta
would also keep sighing through the night, just the way I did. Of
course, God had been unjust to me. But unlike me, Seeta had
been endowed with good looks and buoyant health. He had milk-
white complexion and was quite handsome and attractive to look
at. As his pockets were empty, too, who would have cast him a
second look?

Finally, we decided to settle for two *filmi* friends. Their
attraction was enough to whet the appetites, as both were real
pearls from the kingdom of Lord *Indra*. My friend was known as
Nargis. Her laughter was just like fresh buds in full bloom. She
had large, lotus eyes. The moment she broke into a dance, my
heart would go leaping out of itself. And when she cried, my eyes
would turn moist as well. After seeing two of her movies, so
mesmerised was I of her that later every time her movie was on, I
would go bounding to see it, almost every day of the week.

While watching the movie, I would suddenly stagger on
to my feet, breaking into a loud, heart-rending wail. Only when
Seeta forced me to sit down again, holding me by my arm would

I come to my senses. The people sitting around would laugh and snigger. The label of the 'lover boy' had come unstuck. But I was not an unfaithful lover. Besides, if a lover runs away, scared of people's jibes, he isn't good enough to be a lover at all! You know how difficult it is to be a true lover. They say -

'Everyone can play the lover, donning a turban askew?

Only a few who die, in the distant land of love do arrive.'

So that is how the intensity of my passion grew by the day. Then hell broke loose, all over again. As it is, my heart would keep chanting the name of Nargis all the time. I would often think to myself when would the time come for me to be united with her. Though I knew very well, that someone, who had been rejected even by the ordinary maids, could hardly ever hope to catch her eye. But I was her lover, after all. So how did it matter whether or not she cast even a fleeting glance towards me? Seeta would often tell me that all these *filmi* people lived in Mumbai. He also told me that one way rail fare to Mumbai was no more than forty or fifty rupees. It was his mention of the fare that had weakened my resolve, at least, momentarily. Then I thought to myself, 'Am I so useless that I can't even put together a few rupees for the fare whereas *Mahiwaal,* the legendary lover, is known to have forded the river in spate.

So that's how I thought of making plans to leave for Mumbai. Only a few days back, I had got my salary. I had about ten rupees in my pocket, but the shortfall was in the range of fifty or sixty rupees. I spent one whole night, thinking about the shortfall. Finally, my evil impulses got the better of me. What else could I do? After all, I didn't have any landed property that I could sell off and go. The next day, in the evening, Hari gave me forty rupees to be handed over to the milkman. But I pocketed the money and boarded a train that very night. Night I spent in Bathinda, away from the prying eyes, and the next morning, before the crack of dawn, I got into a train leaving for Delhi. Time and again, all kinds of fears assailed me. And each time, I told myself that no

one could even dream of where I was headed. Seeta was perhaps the only one who would ever get to know of it, and he was,
all said and done, my friend and companion. He could always be
trusted for not disclosing it to anyone.

But once I had found myself a seat in the train, all such
thoughts vanished from my mind. I didn't even realise when the
train arrived in Mumbai. Looking out of the window, I had the
first few glimpses of this great city. Towering buildings and flashing lights. Motor cars and their dazzling lights — shimmering like
the eyes of Nargis. I wondered what kind of *haveli* must she be
living in? ...She would probably have an army of servants around.
It's quite possible that she might be stepping out, only in *purdah*.
So what? She can't stay indoors all the time. She has to step out,
after all. And I wasn't going to kidnap her, either. Lovers are only
afflicted with a longing! Somehow if I manage to get a fleeting
glimpse of hers, my mission would be accomplished. Lost in such
thoughts, I drifted into sleep. I was still riding in the motor cars
when someone suddenly came and shook me, rudely. When I
opened my eyes, I found that three policemen were standing, en-
circling me, handcuffs dangling in their hands. That did make me
lose my nerve momentarily, but then I told myself, 'O heart of
mine, you're not fated to have a glimpse of Nargis; for you, it's
only the handcuffs.'

I don't know which station it was, Rohtak or some other,
but that's where they made the 'lover boy' get off the train. And
the very next day, they had put me behind the bars. Now Puran
Chand started looking around, almost like a vulture. Hari, Seeta
and several other friends came to visit but they didn't leave until
they had rubbed salt in my open wounds. No one so much as
mentioned Nargis' name. And the 'lover boy' lay there, writhing
in pain.

During the second hearing itself, I was awarded three
months of rigorous imprisonment. Now what should I tell you?
Everything of mine was lost in the jail. Puran Chand went flying
out of the bars and so did Nargis. As for the rest of the world, it

had changed already.

When I came out of the jail, I was a changed man. All through the day, standing close to the bridge over the tributary, away from the prying eyes, all I did was cry my heart out, bitterly. I entered the town only once the darkness had descended. At each step, I seemed to falter. My fear was that if someone were to spot me, the earth might just give way under my feet. By the time I finally came to meet Seeta, I was really in a terrible state. I knocked at the door of his *kothri,* but the moment he recognised my voice, he, too, decided not to respond. While walking back, my feet had become as heavy as lead and I could barely lift them. Somehow, I managed to reach the station. That was the last time I boarded a train from that town, as I have never been able to go back there.

Now for the past five years, I've been living in this Bathinda town. But this is hardly the kind of life one wants to lead! I have done every conceivable thing that one could. I just had this single thought helping me through everything; that neither I belong to this world nor does this world belong to me. From stealing to duping and playing the pimp, I have tried out everything. People use all kinds of labels to describe me, a drunkard, a wastrel, a notorious lout, but nothing seems to affect now.

Besides, now my health is also failing me. My limbs have lost their strength. I have lost my hair and more than half of my teeth as well.

Though I lead a very carefree life, occasionally, a deep sense of sadness does overtake me. Especially when it occurs to me that the same person who, we often claim, is worth more than millions or billions, is in absence of money treated as worthless as a torn shirt. Had I been born into a rich family, I, too, would have had a large, extended family of my own by now. There are people who were born paupers but became *Shahs* right before my eyes. They managed to find for themselves beautiful brides as well, that too, as late as forty. And now they are enjoying all the comforts of life.

Sometimes, I think that death is certainly to be preferred

over this kind of wretched life. But somehow, I don't even wish to
die. My friends do sometimes tell me in a state of drunkenness,
'Puran Chand! Don't you worry! It's not long before our time
comes.' Listening to them, I just want to enjoy a quiet laugh up
my sleeves. This kind of kite-flying is what they indulge in, all the
time.

Then I think to myself, why wait for the times when people
like us would have an upper hand and why not, instead live fully
this very moment of which we are a part. Anyway, our death is
not going to leave a gaping void in this country. But take it from
us, the people who have denied us the blessings of marriage are
definitely going to suffer in the fires of hell. After all, the curse of
the saint-lovers such as us won't go unheeded. A bachelor's curse
can even set a boulder on fire, what are men in comparison! ...My
friend Dharma sometimes says – "Purana.... God lives in the eyes,
So not very far from you he is!"

And I often tell him, 'Why, do I want his compassion now
when all my life he just didn't bother for me? Let him live in the
eyes or wherever he wants.

But to tell you honestly, this Dharma is quite a headache.
He is an illiterate person but I don't know where he picks up all
his words of wisdom from. One day, he tells me, 'Now you just
wait and see, how the wheel turns a full circle!' I started laughing.
He tells me, 'Don't laugh, there is going to be some miracle. And
then the tide will turn for you and me....'

Anyway, *janab*, let's see when the prophecy of the
'camel' actually does come true. But as of now, it's only that
proverb in which the jackal proclaims, 'After I'm gone from this
world, it's deluge.' All my limbs are sagging already. So even if
something were to change for me tomorrow, 'how will forty kilos
of milk make any difference to a heifer?' But then you know, Sir,
'there is hope so long as there is life.' Who doesn't want to have
a good life? But who is going to really own us up?

All right, *janab*, jabbering is something you can't really
stop once you start off. If we ever run into each other again in life,

we'll hopefully share our joys and sorrows, again. And if 'we' happen to die, so much the better for God and this world — hardly an asset, I'm only a great burden upon this earth. Not that I've been of any help to anyone ever! ...All right, Sir, I take leave for the time being. *Ram Sat!*

Signed by Puran Chand

In My Own Hand

About The Author

GURDIAL SINGH, recipient of the prestigious Jnanpith Award for 1999, is a contemporary Punjabi novelist and a storyteller par excellence. For him, story telling is not just an art or a craft, but an entire way of life. Small wonder that his own life reads somewhat like a piece of fiction. Born into a family of artisans in the Malwa region, he spent his early years smelting and moulding iron sheets, which he sometimes did for as many as eighteen hours a day. It was his school teacher who encouraged him to resume his studies. After a while it paid off... from teacher to lecturer and then a professor at the Regional Centre of Punjabi University, Patiala. Though he had started his literary career by writing a short story in 1958, success came to him as a novelist when he published his first novel *Marhi Da Deeva* in 1964. Translated into English as *The Last Flicker* (Sahitya Akademi), it was hailed as a modern Indian classic. This was followed by an array of significant long fiction such as *Anhoe* (1966), *Addh Chanini Raat* (1972), *Anhe Ghore Da Daan* (1976) and *Parsa* (1991).

Alongside he continued to nurture his first love for short fiction, and has so far produced as many as eight collections. The notable ones among these are *Saggi Phul* (1962), *Kutta Te Aadmi* (1971), *Begana Pindh* (1985) and *Kareer Di Dhingri* (1991).

Apart from nine novels, he has authored three plays, two prose works, nine books for children and an autobiography in two volumes. Not only has he translated several of his own works into Hindi, but also those of the other reputed Indian and non-Indian writers into Punjabi. Besides *Marhi Da Deeva*, two of his novels *Addh Chanini Raat (Night of the Half-Moon)* (Macmillan, 1996) and *Parsa* (NBT, 2000) are also available in English rendering. Modest to a fault, Gurdial Singh has won countless awards and honours, both national and international, prominent among these being *Sahitya Akademi Award* (1976), *Punjabi Sahitya Akademi Award* (1979), *Soviet Land Nehru Award* (1986) and *Bhai Veer Singh Fiction Award* (1992). After having retired from active teaching, he lives at Jaito, his home town, and devotes all his time to reading and writing.

ABOUT THE TRANSLATOR

RANA NAYAR, born in 1957 at Amritsar, Taught at St. Bede's College, Shimla, from 1980 to 1990, before joining the Department of English, Punjab University, Chandigarh, in 1990, where he is currently teaching. A critic, scholar and translator, he has translated two of Gurdial Singh's novels viz. *Night of the Half Moon* (1996) and *Parsa* (NBT, 2000). A Charles Wallace Indian Trust Awardee for 1999, he has also won the commendation award for translation from British Council and Katha. His forthcoming publications are: *From Across the Shores* (2002), a collection of stories by UK based Punjabi writers in English translation; *Edward Albee: Towards a Typology of Human Relationships* (New Delhi) and *The Eye of a Doe* (New Delhi), a collection of *Mohan Bhandari's Short Stories in English Translation.* He is currently working on a postdoctoral project titled: (Mis) *readings of The Mahabharata: Ideology, Narrative, History and Culture.* Apart from translation, he is actively involved in theatre and has directed some dozen odd plays and acted on half a dozen as well. As a bilingul, who writes in Hindi and English he regularly contributes articles/reviews to *The Tribune, The Indian Express, The Book Review, The Pioneer; The Hindu, Dainik Bhaskar, New Quest, Summerhill IIAS Review* and *Pal Pratipal* et al.